CAROLINE: CASE SIXTEEN

A LT. KATE GAZZARA NOVEL

THE LT. KATE GAZZARA MURDER FILES
BOOK 16

BLAIR HOWARD

For Jo, as always.

1

November 30

Saturday morning, 6:25 a.m.

JEFF HARPER'S PICKUP JOLTED OVER THE UNEVEN grass track. He swore and stepped on the clutch hard, ground the gears, then got himself right again. Through the windshield, the blaze of light on the horizon made it hard to see where he was going. But he was more than familiar with these surroundings.

He'd passed the battered cemetery sign about five hundred feet back, and the trees were beginning to close in around him. The cemetery itself was half a mile off the main road and poorly maintained despite still being used for *new* residents.

His wife was buried in one of the first rows, where the gravestones weren't eaten away by weather and the dry summer air. He visited her religiously every Saturday morning before opening up the auto repair shop at 7:30 sharp.

The truck lurched over a hump of dirt and knotted grass. He threw it in neutral, yanked up the parking brake, and stepped out into the cool Tennessee morning air.

A quick glance at his watch told him that he had to make it fast; he was running late and it was a half-hour drive back to the shop.

Purely out of habit, he scanned the tree line looking for nothing in particular but, to the west, the cemetery was just a short distance from Booker T. Washington State Park, where he and his wife Lauren used to hike.

Jeff sighed and started toward her headstone, hands in his pockets, head down, halfway depressed. Lauren, the victim of a car accident, a spin-out during an uncharacteristic winter squall, the roads slick with snow that was melting quickly, had passed three years prior, but he still missed her. An SUV had hit Lauren's little Volkswagen and sent her right over the guardrail into a ditch. She'd been only twenty-seven at the time, and three years later Jeff still came to the cemetery to talk to her.

"Dang," he muttered, stopping dead in his tracks, then turning and jogging back toward the truck. He'd forgotten the peonies, Lauren's favorite. Dipping a hand in through the window to grab them, he turned again and then, out of the corner of his eye, he saw something, a pickup truck; there was someone else in the cemetery, which was highly unusual, especially at that time in the morning.

The cemetery was old and out of the way, remote almost, to the point where few new people wanted to be interred there. Those that did were interred by special request. In Lauren's case, her grandparents were there and she'd loved the area. That being said, Jeff couldn't remember ever, *ever* seeing anyone else there at 6:30 in the morning; not in the three years since the funeral.

But there it was. A blue Dodge pickup parked close to the tree line, on the western edge of the cemetery, almost invisible in the early morning shadows. Windows rolled up, engine off.

The trees swayed in a late-fall breeze—November 30 —cooling the meadowy area, but a shiver went down Jeff's spine for another reason. With the peonies resting against his thigh, he realized that it was too still; nothing other than the treetops was moving. With a glance at Lauren's gravestone, Jeff placed the peonies a few feet away and started toward the truck, high-kneeing it through the tall grass that the groundskeeper had yet to deal with.

"Hey," he called out, pulse pounding in his head. Something was wrong, and he wished now that he'd grabbed a tire iron out of the back of his truck. "Hey!" he called again. "You okay there?"

Squinting, he thought from that distance that the front seat looked empty. *Probably a bench seat*, he thought, categorizing the truck as a beat-up '77. No one answered.

7

"I'm just going to take a look," he murmured aloud, half to himself and half to Lauren. If she were here, she'd be shaking her head, telling him not to be a fool. But Jeff couldn't just pick up and leave. What if someone was hurt? Overdosed? Having a heart attack? "Just in case I need to call Brad," he continued quietly, thinking of the old groundskeeper he had little contact with.

Brad certainly didn't work himself to death keeping the little cemetery neat and tidy, but he was a good man, and respectful. When Lauren's peonies dried up, he disposed of them and put fresh water in the vase. And Jeff was sure that, if needed, Brad would have the truck towed and find the owners.

He continued through the long grass, leaning to the right to try and see around the truck. There was a patch of flattened grass near the driver's side rear wheel. The trees swayed and shadows played over the windshield.

"Anyone in there?" Jeff called, the hair on the back of his neck prickling.

A sporadic rustling broke the silence of the morning and he froze.

A branch near the ground bounced, and a squirrel bounded out, twitching its tail at the sight of the human and quickly making off toward the towering oaks.

Exhaling with relief, Jeff started forward purposefully. *If I don't hurry, I'm going to be late, and Steve doesn't have a key to the office door. Got to make time today to have a copy made.* His mind wandered through a mundane checklist as he approached the truck.

He'd started the automotive business just a year after

he and Lauren got married, and it had taken off. At the time, it'd seemed like things were taking a turn for the better. Maybe she'd be able to stop working such long shifts at the hospital, take a break and hunker down at home to raise their kids. He'd been so excited to start a family with her. Just the morning of the accident, she'd laughed at him as she tossed out her birth control, giving him a saucy grin.

Up close now, he was sure the truck was a '77. Despite the faded paint and a cracked side mirror, the wheels were in excellent condition. Someone loved this vehicle.

Jeff stood on the balls of his feet and peered into the driver's side window. He gasped, stumbling backward, his heel catching on a clod of dirt and sending him sprawling. Crawling quickly backward, he tried to process what he'd just seen.

It was a minute and a half-dozen deep breaths before he approached the truck again to confirm what he thought he'd seen.

Slumped sideways over on the bench seat was a blonde-headed girl, arms dangling at her sides. He couldn't see her face because of how she was positioned— just the tip of her upturned nose. And blood. A lot of blood.

It was all over the dash and the back of the bench seat, splattered across the rear window. And on the seat under her head... a dark pool, congealed, like deer blood when it was left to stand in a bucket.

Jeff inhaled deeply and took a step back. His cell

phone was already in his hand, and as he thumbed through his contacts, he moved around the truck, careful to stay at least four or five feet away from it. *This has to be a crime scene*, he thought.

Holding the phone to his ear, he listened to it ring and ring before a generic voicemail came on. With a grunt, he hung up and hit "call" again. And then, as he backed around the bed of the truck, he found another body.

The tailgate was down, and he could see two feet clad in beat-up Nikes sticking out over the edge, the long legs clad in jeans. He took another step back and stared at the supine body of a boy with dark hair, his arms spread, eyes wide staring up at the trees, shadows of the branches moving back and forth across his face, making it look almost as if he was alive, but...

And there was a lot of blood, and he stood there, staring in horror at the blood that had dripped from the tailgate onto the grass, already thickening in the cool, early morning air; dark, ink-like blots.

"Brad," Jeff choked into the phone as he staggered backward away from the truck and its ghastly contents, "it's Jeff Harper. I'm at the cemetery. You need to get down here. There's a body. There's two bodies. I'm calling the cops."

He stared, unblinking, at the Dodge as the groundskeeper tried to pry information out of him, but Jeff's brain had stalled. He could barely think. He turned and began to run, stumbling back to Lauren's grave. The peonies crunched under his boots. He stopped, turned again to gaze at the blue pickup and dialed 911.

The dispatcher's voice was cool, her tone measured, professional, and he was instantly taken back to the phone call he'd gotten the day Lauren had died in the crash. And, as he tried to calmly explain what he'd found, depression and dismay descended upon him.

2

Saturday morning, 7:35 a.m.

As usual, Samson was kicking my butt on our morning run. The cool, early morning air was refreshing, but I could feel the sweat prickling along my hairline as my ponytail bounced against the back of my neck. Sammy was huffing contentedly along a few paces ahead of me.

I didn't usually let him off-leash, but he was more than familiar with that particular trail and had excellent recall.

After the last case, I'd agreed to take a little time off. Well, I say agreed; Chief Johnston insisted, but what it really meant was working regular, forty-hour weeks instead of my normal sixty to seventy. It also meant more time for exercising Sammy, who needed *a lot* of exercise.

We had a lot in common, me and Sam. Both couch potatoes when we weren't working—and balls of energy when we were. I couldn't have asked for a better partner and, now that we were closing on a house that week, it finally felt like I was settling down a little.

Samson disappeared around a corner and I kicked it up a notch to catch up with him. I didn't like him being out of my sight. Not that I didn't trust him. I did; I do. Was I getting too attached to him? Yes, for sure, and every time we went for a run and he darted away for a few moments... well, I was anxious: no apologies.

But that morning... maybe it wasn't just Sammy taking off to terrorize a squirrel that alerted my senses. Shooting him a glance, I passed him quickly, and he stood there looking agonizingly from me to the tree he was guarding, before choosing me. He took off after me, kicking up the gravel on the trail, mouth open and tongue lolling, and I couldn't help grinning at him.

It was unusual for us to go running on a Saturday. I'd changed my schedule to accommodate the chief and my team. Sunday through Thursday, I worked my butt off. Fridays I took it easy. Saturdays were my "cheat" days when Sammy and I would share a burger or just lounge around in the morning and catch up on some mindless TV show. It did my mind good just to relax and forget the rigors of the Homicide Division. But that morning, I hadn't been able to help myself; I was, for some reason, antsy.

I'd woken up at just after four o'clock and stared at the red glow of the alarm clock. Then I lay there staring up at the ceiling until the dim light of dawn began to appear on the horizon and I got up and convinced Samson to do so, too.

A couple of weeks earlier, I'd shifted him off my bed onto an orthopedic dog bed that cost almost as much as my queen mattress. At first, he wasn't happy about it, but after the first night, he'd taken to it surprisingly well and it was hard to get him up. But when he saw me putting on my sneakers, he upped and beat it to the door.

I remember the restless, sick feeling I had as I drove to the greenway. I also remember that Samson had whined on the passenger seat next to me, seemingly able to sense my unrest. Even after fifteen minutes into a fast run, sweat running down my spine, I wasn't able to completely shake the feeling that something was wrong.

I'd had the feeling before; a kind of knotted nausea, a hollow sensation deep in the pit of my gut, eating away at me. A feeling of impending doom.

My last big case—the murder of Indigo Salazar—had left me more shaken up than usual. Why, I wasn't sure; maybe it was the multiple layers of betrayal involved. Or the fact that her death could have been avoided had she not made so many bad choices. But isn't that what teenagers do, make bad choices? And I'm sure you've heard the saying, "When a butterfly flaps its wings in the Amazonian rain forest..." If you haven't, here's the quote from Catherine McKenzie—*Fractured*.

"They say that if a butterfly flaps its wings in the Amazonian rain forest, it can change the weather half a world away. Chaos theory. What it means is that everything that happens in this moment is an accumulation of everything that's come before it. Every breath. Every thought. There is no innocent action. Some actions end up having the force of a tempest. Their impact cannot be missed. Others are the blink of an eye. Passing by unnoticed. Perhaps only God knows which is which."

All I know today is that you can think that what you've done is only the flap of a butterfly wing, when it's really a thunderclap, and both can result in a hurricane."

Thought-provoking, don't you think? I do, and it was what came to my mind as I sucked air in through my nose, ignoring the stitch in my side.

Anne Robar, a member of my team, had been trying to convince me to check out therapy and talk to someone about my anxiety, if that's what it was. Me? I didn't think so and was resistant to the idea. But on mornings like that one, when something was eating away at my gut... Well, as usual, I shrugged it off, putting it down to intuition and almost twenty years on the job.

"All right, boy." I sighed, slowing to a foot-dragging pace and clicking my tongue. Samson made a big loop, turned back toward me at a lope, and folded at my feet. I squinted up at the sky. It was going to be another beautiful day in Chattanooga: sunny, crisp and cold, with winter less than a month away.

I stood for a moment, bent over, hands on my knees, head down, breathing hard. And then my phone buzzed.

I looked at Samson. His dark brown eyes met mine. He tilted his head sideways, looking up at me as if he felt it too: doom and gloom.

I glanced at the screen. It was Chief Johnston. *Shit! I just knew it.*

What did I know? I was a Captain, and a homicide detective, after all, and Johnston only assigned me to the most serious cases. And he never called me unless something was up.

"Chief?"

"Good morning, Kate," he said. "I'm not disturbing you, I hope."

"Not at all. I'm out on the Greenway with Samson. What's up?" I asked, clipping Samson's leash onto his harness. He panted, looking up at me expectantly. We had a three-mile run back to the parking lot. I gave the leash a little tug and started walking. There was no doubt I'd be heading in to work.

Chief Wesley Johnston had been running things at the Chattanooga PD for more than thirty years, much longer than I'd been a cop, and we had a... somewhat precarious relationship based on mutual annoyance and respect. I annoyed him, and he respected the results I got, even if I didn't always get them the way he wanted me to. My last case, for example. Chief Johnston hadn't been thrilled with how I'd handled Ivan Salazar, the victim's socially prominent father. But I caught his daughter's killer as well as a string of criminals involved in drug and human trafficking.

"I'm sorry, Kate, but I need you at a crime scene."

I nodded, then remembered where I was—in the park, early morning, no one around except for the birds and a lone jogger way off in the distance.

"Right," I said. "I'll get on over there, but first I need to go home and change. Where is it and what is it? Can you give me a heads-up?" I stopped walking and bent into a stretch, feeling my muscles cramping. That's what I got for rushing into the run and not stretching beforehand.

"Booker T. Washington State Park. Two bodies at a nearby cemetery. Both homicides."

I frowned. "Booker T? That's outside our jurisdiction."

"The park itself is, yes. But the cemetery is inside the city limits, which makes it our problem. Your problem."

I breathed in deeply through my nose as Johnston filled me in on the only details they had at that point.

"I'm told," he said, "that the bodies are those of a male and a female. Both appear to be in their teens. They were found by a man visiting his wife's grave. He noticed a vehicle parked at the back end of the cemetery. It's a pretty remote area, Kate. Mike Willis and Doc Sheddon are on their way there now. You need to be there too."

"This early?" I asked. "How did you manage that? Doc doesn't usually start before eight-thirty."

"He was already at the Forensic Center taking care of last night's fire victim, and Willis is heading there from home, I believe. Just get over there, Kate. I'll text you the address. I haven't called Corbin yet, but I'll do it now," Johnston said. "But you're heading on over there now, right?"

"I am," I said breathlessly, already starting a warm-up jog back toward the parking lot. Sammy pulled anxiously at the leash, as if he knew we had work to do. "As soon as I've changed my clothes. Thanks, Chief."

"Of course, Captain," he replied. "Keep me informed."

"Don't I always?" I asked.

"When it suits you, yes," he replied. "Talk to you later."

He hung up, and Sammy and I sped up into an all-out run, feeling the mood of doom and gloom burn off as I ran, to be replaced by one of grim determination.

As I ran, blind to my surroundings, the few facts Johnston had given me whirled through my mind. Two bodies, teens, in a cemetery close to a state park. I was familiar with Booker T. Washington, having spent time there when I was a youngster. *What had those two kids been up to? Hooking up? Hiking? Just having some alone time?*

The irony of the situation didn't escape me. Two bodies in a cemetery. *Yep, that's another first.*

As I thought about it, that weird feeling in the pit of my gut returned. *Is this the doom I've been sensing? And the gloom? In less than half an hour, I'll be knee-deep in unnatural death, loss, grief...*

As soon as we reached the SUV, Sammy jumped up into the backseat and stood on the center console as if he was navigating our way home.

My apartment sparked a sense of detachment in me now that I knew this was our last week in it. I'd miss this funny little home, the space I'd grown so used to, but I was also excited for new beginnings.

Swinging the door open, I told Sammy, "Better eat quick and catch your breath. We've got places to be, boy."

I walked carefully along the short hallway, avoiding the packed boxes. In four days, if everything went well, the paperwork would be signed and I'd have the keys to a cute little bungalow in a quiet residential area of Chattanooga. Samson would have a fenced-in quarter-acre and some quiet streets where we could go for walks on lazy days.

But I expected it to take at least a few weeks to move everything in. The amount of *stuff* I had was surprising.

After a quick five-minute shower to wash off the sweat, I threw on a long-sleeved gray shirt, my second-best pair of jeans, and my boots. As an afterthought, I grabbed a dark red leather jacket on the way out, too. It was late November and already turning chilly. The sun was up. The forecast was good. But I wasn't convinced it would get any warmer.

3

SAMSON WASN'T HAPPY ABOUT BEING LEFT IN THE car so, after several heart-wrenching barks, muffled by the car windows, I opened the back door and let him out. He jumped down and, at the sight of the surrounding woodlands, immediately perked up. I grabbed my to-go cup of coffee from the cup holder and together, with Samson on a tight leash, we walked the hundred feet down the road to where more than a dozen officers, and my partner Corbin, were waiting.

The somewhat overgrown driveway into the cemetery, though calling it that was being generous, had been blocked off with yellow crime scene tape. A sweeping look around the area told me it was a little-used cemetery, which was not surprising since it was out in the middle of nowhere.

Most people preferred to be interred in the county's

rolling, well-kept residential cemeteries or the city's practical grid-like layouts. But as a breeze rustled the oaks and maples, I understood the draw of this particular cemetery. It was quiet out there. Serene. Private.

"Sergeant," I greeted Corbin, shooting the officers securing the scene a polite smile as well. "The chief gave me a quick run-down, but what are we looking at here?"

Corbin cleared his throat, clutching his to-go cup close to his chest, and looked down meaningfully at Samson. The oversized pup would probably have loved a romp in the grassy cemetery, but who knew what evidence might be scattered among the headstones? I moved toward one of the officers standing guard at the tapes.

"Do you mind?" I asked, holding Sammy's leash out to him. The officer—his tag bore the name A. Milner—nodded politely and took Sam, giving him a good rub between the ears. Samson whined, realizing I wasn't going to let him go with me.

I took a sip of the hot coffee and heaved a sigh of pleasure. Corbin smiled and then proceeded to answer my question.

"A man named Jeff Harper was visiting his wife's grave when he found the victims," Corbin said as we set off at a leisurely pace along the worn, uneven drive. The grass on either side was shin and knee-high, but up ahead I could just make out headstones poking up.

"That must have been tough for him," I said absently, looking this way and that as we walked, trying to get a feel for the place.

"Yeah. Gruesome," he replied. "His wife passed three years ago. He said he rarely sees anyone out here, especially at half-past six in the morning, but he noticed a truck parked at the edge of the cemetery, and that seemed off to him. So he decided to check it out, and that's when he found the bodies."

I nodded, everything lining up with what Johnston had already told me in our clipped conversation.

"He's still here, I take it," I said.

"Yep. That's him, over there, by his truck." Corbin pointed to a tall, lanky man with dark hair that was starting to thin on top. He had a phone to his ear and was holding a baseball cap in his other hand with the logo *Harper's Auto* above the bill.

"He's younger than I expected. Who's he talking to?" I asked. I didn't like witnesses making phone calls from a crime scene. You never knew what sensitive information they might be giving away, or to whom.

Jeff Harper didn't look like the kind of person to spread gossip, but one can never be too careful.

He finished his conversation and stared blankly at the cell phone in his hand.

"He said he wanted to talk to his therapist," Corbin replied. "He, uh... He seems to be struggling a bit, but he agreed to stick around until you got here."

I nodded, adjusted the holster on my belt, and then walked over to him. He glanced at me, did a double take, then looked at Corbin, who introduced me.

"Mr. Harper," he began, "this is Captain Gazzara. She's the lead investigating officer."

Harper looked at me and nodded, but said nothing.

"Hello, Mr. Harper," I said, looking around his pickup truck. I could see a rosary hanging from the rearview mirror. "Please tell me exactly what happened here; how you discovered the bodies. What time did you get here? What time did you find the bodies? Begin at the beginning. Don't leave anything out."

Harper took a deep breath, closed his eyes, then seemed to crumple in on himself. He glanced at one of the newer gravestones nearby, whereon lay a bouquet of squashed peonies as pale as his face.

"It was around six-thirty when I got here," he began. "I stop by every Saturday morning to see my wife. I'd been here about ten minutes, I guess, when I... When I saw the truck and—" He shook his head and trailed off.

"Mr. Harper?" I said, then took a sip of coffee to take the edge off my impatience.

I could understand the difficulty he was having and the stress he was dealing with, but what I needed was for the man to tell his story. I needed to get a jump on whatever had happened there.

He hesitated, coughed, and looked away. *Geez!* I thought and pursed my lips.

"Please continue," I said. "What was so unusual about the pickup that it attracted your attention? I take it you'd never seen it before, or... what?"

He shook his head, then put his cap back on. "No. Nothing. There's never anyone here that early, not even many during the day. Which is why it stood out to me. I thought maybe it was teenagers fooling around, or... someone under the influence of something."

He choked up. I glanced at Corbin who, as usual, was looking pityingly at him.

I almost shook my head and rolled my eyes, but I didn't. I also knew the interview wasn't going well. I needed more, so I decided to push him harder.

"You're sure you didn't see anyone, anyone who might have done this?"

He shook his head and said, "No. After I found... I looked around, but there was no one."

"Did you touch anything?" I asked.

Again he shook his head, then said, "No... I don't think so." Which probably meant that he had.

"How often do you come here?" I asked.

"Every Saturday."

"And for how long?"

He rubbed at his eyes, then blinked hard when he took his hand away. "Three years. Lauren passed three years ago in an accident."

"I'm sorry for your loss," I said.

He nodded, still looking around anxiously. His attitude was setting my radar off, but I couldn't tell if he was just a guy who was still knee-deep in grief at the loss of his wife or if there was something strange going on.

I handed him my card and said, "Mr. Harper, I know you're having a hard time with this, but we're going to need a full statement. I'll have one of my officers take it. In the meantime, we're going to hang onto your truck for a while. D'you have a way to get home?"

"Yes, I called my—"

The radio on Corbin's belt crackled. He turned away, the radio to his ear, then he turned to Harper and said, "Your buddy is here. Out front. Officer McCarty will escort you out."

"One more thing before you go," I said. "If you think of anything else, please call me. I'll contact you if we need you again."

He nodded, turned away, and the serious-faced Officer McCarty walked with him back toward the cemetery entrance. His truck would remain with us until Mike Willis cleared it.

"What do you think?" I asked Corbin.

He took a sip of coffee before answering. "The guy's obviously shaken up. A little off his rocker, maybe, but I don't think he had anything to do with what happened here. That would be kind of weird, though, right? To kill someone in your wife's own cemetery?"

I agreed, but Jeff Harper wasn't doing himself any favors with the way he was acting. Then again, grief could do strange things to people. Turn them into something they weren't born to be.

"You want to take a look at the scene?" Corbin asked. "Talk to Doc Sheddon?"

"Yes. But let me take a look around here first."

I could see that Mike Willis' people had already begun to process Harper's truck and the surrounding area. They'd even marked the peonies. I stepped closer to the grave. The headstone had the name Lauren Harper on it. The inscription was surprisingly long.

You will remember
when this is blown over
and everything's all by the way
when I grow older
I'll be there at your side
to remind you
How I still love you.
I still love you.

Damn! That's poignant. I thought as I looked at Corbin. He had a somber expression on his face. There was no doubt that Jeff Harper and his wife had had something special going, and I was kind of envious—not of the grave—of what they had.

"Oh, hey. Sorry. I just need to..." A young guy in nerdy glasses stumbled up next to me and snapped a quick photo of the gravestone and peonies. He dipped into his pocket, pulled out a recording device, and spoke into it: "Ten feet from pickup truck; headstone reading 'Lauren Harper.' Peonies allegedly left by husband, Jeffery Harper."

He stowed the device away in his pocket, then snapped more photos as I watched, stunned, wondering who the hell he was and what the hell he thought he was doing.

He finally turned to me and introduced himself, "Hi. I'm Aubrey Pugh. I'm the department's new photographer."

"Hi," I replied slowly, holding out a hand that he shook with the loose enthusiasm of youth. My brows rose and I heard Corbin cough somewhere nearby.

"Captain Kate Gazzara, right?" Pugh said lightly. "I think we'll be seeing each other a lot. I, um, I have to get to it. This crime scene stuff. This is only my third gig."

Abruptly, he turned and high-kneed it away toward the far end of the cemetery, where Doc Sheddon was hustling around the victim's truck.

I watched the kid go, shaking my head.

"He's gotta be, what, all of twenty-three, twenty-four?" I said.

"Probably. There about. But hey, he's enthusiastic, right?"

"Yeah, that," I said dryly. More like a constant, buzzing energy that I knew I'd find annoying soon enough. But I tried to focus on the positives; Corbin was right. Having an enthusiastic, quick but thorough addition to the team was always a win.

Doc was brushing off his almost-white coat and chatting to three ME students who were doing field training.

"Ah," he said, interrupting himself and gesturing to me enthusiastically and eyeing my coffee cup. "Captain! Perfect timing. I was just going to go over the scene piece-by-piece with the students, if you'd like to listen in."

I nodded a hello and stayed off to the side, ears perked but eyes on the truck. The driver's side door was only a few feet away and from the angle at which I was positioned, I saw what appeared to be a spray of blood on the dash...

"As you can see, we have two victims here. A female between the age of fifteen and eighteen, though I'd personally guess that she's closer to eighteen, and a male somewhere in the same age range. The female was shot where she sat in the passenger side of the vehicle. The bullet entered through the passenger side window and passed out through the driver's side door."

A quick glance nearby told me that Willis and his team had projected the probable trajectory and were searching the ground for said bullet.

"Doc, excuse me," I interrupted. "Was this close range, or..."

Doc perked up, rocking back and forth on his heels while making a pleased sound. "Excellent question, Captain. Excellent. As you'll see here..." He stepped carefully around the side of the truck, and the students, as well as me and Corbin, followed him.

Doc pointed to the passenger window with a pencil. It was rolled a little more than halfway down and the top edge of the glass had a large chip in it.

"The bullet actually clipped the top of the window, here—just enough to leave a mark—before coming into contact with our victim. She died almost instantly. It was a clean shot. I'd say from long-range."

I turned and stared out into the woods, toward the state park. What the heck had happened here? Long range? In the dark? That's one hell of a shot. It was then that I remembered: there'd been a half moon that night.

"...a rifle of some sort," Doc continued. "The second shot entered at an angle and created the majority of the blood splatter you see on the dash. Our second victim..."

Doc shuffled around, huffing as he struggled through the tall grass and out of the shade. I realized I'd completely missed the body in the back of the truck bed, probably because it was already covered with a sheet. I'd assumed that, like the girl, the boy would have been shot while in the vehicle.

"...was shot in the neck. A perfect shot."

Doc, as usual, sounded almost gleeful as he described the cause of death. One of the students—a tall kid of about twenty-four—looked like he was going to be sick.

Corbin leaned closer, looking into the truck bed as Doc carefully lifted the sheet. "What, I wonder, was he doing out here in the open?" he asked, as I was asking myself the same question.

Clearing his throat, the rotund medical examiner gestured and said, "I don't think this, here"—he pointed to heavy spatter on the kid's jacket—"is his blood. I'm almost sure of it, though we'll have to test it to be certain. I believe he was in the vehicle when his companion was shot, and then he got out, probably to run. If you look here"—he lifted the right forearm and pointed—"there's a graze here on his forearm. I think that was made when the bullet that killed the girl passed by him. He was shot outside of the truck and moved here."

Doc turned his attention fully to the students, outlining the body temperatures, the degree of rigor mortis, lividity, the weather, the outside temp, and other details I zoned out on. One of the students, a girl, the only one in the group, correctly asserted that the deaths had taken place between 12 and 1:30 am.

Doc looked pleased; Corbin looked at *me*, and I knew what he was thinking. Jeff Harper would likely not have an alibi for that time in the morning—not unless he was sleeping with someone, which I seriously doubted, remembering his woeful demeanor at the mention of the death of his wife—so we wouldn't be able to quickly rule him out as a suspect. Someone would have to check and try to find out exactly where he was and with whom.

Doc, serious now, glanced around at the students before dismissing them, admonished them to write up their notes and email them to him for evaluation, then turned them loose. They stumbled away as Aubrey Pugh, the crime scene photographer, snapped photos noisily away nearby. How a digital camera could be so loud, I had no idea.

"Kate," Doc began, joining Corbin and me and reaching for my coffee cup, which I reluctantly handed to him, "this is a complicated one. I find it very confusing. As I said, the boy was shot outside of the vehicle. Mike and I have identified blood splatter on an area of grass just over there. And someone... threw him into the truck bed. You can see the blood has pooled beneath his neck and upper body. There's actually a very thin trail that leads from there to the back of the truck, but..." He took a big gulp of coffee.

Dread filled my gut. This wasn't going to be good news.

"But there's not much evidence to help us," Mike Willis, the department's CSI supervisor, said tiredly as he joined us. "This area's just too wild, Kate. I can see that someone wearing boots moved the body, but the grass..." He shook his head. "There are no prints of any kind. No bloody fingerprints or smudges anywhere on the truck that I can tell so far. Whoever did this didn't touch the girl. If they left anything on the boy's clothing, we'll find out once Doc sends them to me. We're looking for bullets. There's a good chance we'll find the one that killed the girl, but the others..." He shook his head. "I'll have the truck transported to the compound. We'll give it a thorough going over. Give me a couple of days, okay?"

I nodded thoughtfully. Willis was a veteran when it came to handling crime scenes. There was little chance he'd miss anything.

"ID?" I asked.

"Not yet," he replied. "We haven't touched the bodies. We're leaving that to Doc."

I nodded.

"Lieutenant Willis?" a voice shouted.

He turned. One of his techs was waving an evidence bag. He gestured for her to join him. I knew Sasha. I'd done martial arts with her for a number of years.

"What have you got, Sasha?" he asked, taking the bag from her. "Hah, a bullet. Looks like a 30-30 to me."

Before he could continue, I felt fine water droplets hit my face and I glanced at Corbin in horror. Willis cursed.

"Go, go," he shooed Sasha back toward the other tech, "get everything secured. I'm going to fetch a tarp from the van. We need to get this truck covered."

He left cursing, fists clenched as he struggled through the tall, quickly dampening grass. The sky had turned a foreboding gray, the light sprinkle was increasing and the breeze picking up, shifting the leaves overhead.

"You okay, Doc?" I asked as he wiped off his half-glasses.

"Oh, yes. We'll be fine. We'll pack 'em up and haul 'em away back to the center."

I closed my eyes and inwardly smiled at his nonchalant approach to... almost everything, but that was Doc. He was a genius when it came to forensic medicine, but he could be a bit crass about the victims. A byproduct of his profession, I supposed.

Me? I totally understood the need to separate oneself from the gruesomeness of it all and so, at least to some extent, I'd grown used to Doc's gallows humor.

"We should get back to the office," Corbin said, clearly not thrilled about the change in weather. "Leave them to it and bring the team up to speed."

I nodded, shielding my face with a hand and taking one last look at the cemetery. It was a wild, beautiful, dark place, and yet it felt... feral.

"Yes," I replied, "but give me a minute, okay? I want to take another look at the bodies."

He nodded, and I snapped on a pair of latex gloves and went to the passenger-side door.

The girl couldn't have known what hit her. She was slumped over to her left, her head at an odd angle. I could see where the bullet entered but not the exit wound. I didn't touch her. Instead I just shook my head. She looked very young, and from what little I could see of her face, pretty, with blonde hair. The inside of the cab was awash with congealing blood and blood spatter. I stood for a moment staring at her then backed away and went around to the truck bed.

I leaned over the side and lifted the sheet. The kid was lying on his back, his eyes wide open, blood pooled around his head. The entry wound was in the left side of his neck. The bullet had passed on through, tearing a hole the size of a walnut on the right side. Judging from the angle, I figured it must have passed through the left carotid artery and the trachea before exiting at the right front.

Whew! What the hell could have possibly happened here? I wondered.

"Let's go," I said, as I lowered the sheet and stepped away.

Corbin nodded, and we walked away back to our cars.

4

Saturday morning, 9:10 a.m.

WHEN WE ARRIVED BACK AT THE CEMETERY entrance, I found Sammy straining at his leash, growling and barking and the officer holding him hanging on for dear life as he tugged at the leash, trying to get to me.

"Hey, boy, it's all right. I'm right here."

"Is he okay?" Corbin asked as I took the leash and wrapped it around my wrist.

"Yes, he's fine," I replied, but I wasn't so sure... the big shepherd was humming deep in his throat, a low growl nobody could hear, but I could feel it vibrating the leash. Something was up, and I began to feel uneasy. If Samson was on edge, there was a good reason. The dog was a scarily accurate judge of character.

He was standing, leaning forward against the leash, staring at a red pickup parked with its driver's window down maybe a hundred feet away from the cemetery entrance. It was a beast. Tricked out, as the kids would say, with insanely wide tires and jacked up at least a couple of feet. Getting up into the cab must have been a real pain in the ass for anyone over the age of thirty.

"Hush, boy," I said, scratching the sweet spot behind his ear. But even that didn't calm him. He emitted another low growl. Another warning? He turned his head, looked up at me and our eyes met. "What is it, Sam?"

He snapped his jaws, licked his nose and continued to look up at me.

I shook my head, turned to McCarty and said, "Go check out that truck."

McCarty nodded and walked quickly away.

I took Samson to my SUV, opened the front passenger door and prompted Samson to jump in. He did, and immediately shook himself. I shut the door gently and, trying to ignore his anxious tip-tapping on the driver's seat, I nodded to Corbin. We followed McCarty to the truck where he was arguing with the driver, and I could tell by the pitch of the person responding that the occupants were young.

"Hey," I said, "I've got it, McCarty. Thank you."

McCarty looked annoyed and relieved. He tipped his hat, then called to his team to make sure the street was blocked off. Something that should've been done earlier.

Stepping up to the truck on the driver's side, I had to crane my neck to see inside. The window was down, a rough-looking elbow hanging out of it and a grinning face looking down on me.

"Can I help you boys?" I asked, just barely able to get a glimpse of the passenger. They both appeared to be in their late teens, early twenties. *Friends of the victims?* I wondered.

"What's going on here, officer?" the kid in the passenger seat asked, leaning forward to look at me.

"Captain," Corbin corrected, obviously not thrilled with the kid's flippant attitude.

"Better watch it, Luke." The driver leaned out of the window, his arm hanging down the door, and smirked. From what little I could see of him, he was well-built, with dark blond hair, young, and looked like a jock but with a country twist. Meaning a bad haircut and a camouflage shirt with the sleeves cut off.

"Hi, ma'am," the driver said, his eyes half closed. "I'm Ben, and this here's Luke. We're just curious about what's going on out here."

Somehow, despite the feigned politeness, I liked Ben even less than Luke.

I ignored the question and said, "This is a police line. You're not supposed to be here. Do you live nearby?"

Ben shook his head, and I didn't miss the look Luke shot him.

"We're just heading for the shooting range, ma'am," Ben replied. "I shoot competition skeet, and Luke is my spotter."

I stared hard at him. There was something about his tone that was rubbing me the wrong way. Corbin shifted, and I heard him flip open his notebook.

"I didn't realize there was a range out here," I said. "You know the area well?"

This time, Luke spoke up first. "Yes ma'am. I live about two miles down the road, and Ben's from town, too. We're out here most every weekend."

"Are you familiar with this cemetery?" Corbin asked.

Luckily the rain had stopped.

"A bit," Ben responded, shooting a quick glance toward the blocked-off entrance. "It's a popular spot for teens, that's for sure."

"Oh? How so?"

The two exchanged a glance. Ben answered again. "Well, you know. Kids like their privacy. What's more private than a cemetery? No one telling secrets there." He smirked again as Luke laughed.

The joke fell flat. I was annoyed. It was the same whenever we had to deal with teenagers: smart-ass answers to questions, disrespect for law enforcement, and these two... well, I just wasn't in the mood.

"Sorry, ma'am," Luke said, apparently catching the look on my face. "Ben can be a bit crass, 'specially when we're going out shooting. But he's right. This is a popular spot for kids to hang out, drink, mess around a bit, you know, right?" His brow furrowed. His brown eyes met mine. "Did you find someone out there?" he asked.

Corbin sipped the last of his coffee loudly, trying to juggle the to-go cup and notepad.

"We'll help however we can," Luke added, politely turning the conversation. "Just ask Ben. He's brought a girl or two out here. Right Ben?" With an infectious grin, he nudged his crew-cut buddy, whose smirk told me everything I needed to know about what he got up to out here. He reminded me of a high school boyfriend I'd had who didn't understand "no."

"I think we're done here," I said, digging into a pocket and taking out one of my cards. I handed it up to Ben. "If you think of anything, if either of you remember seeing anything odd in the area last night, give me a call, please."

"Yes, ma'am," both boys echoed. Ben started up the truck with a roar.

"Hey," Corbin called out. "I need your names, for the record."

"Luke Webber," the passenger said.

"I'm Ben Whitt," the driver answered.

I left Corbin jotting down his notes and headed back to my SUV, squinting to see what Samson was up to. Between the rain and his anxiety, the windows were all fogged up. His tongue cleared a little spot, and as soon as he saw me, he settled back into the passenger seat.

I pulled myself halfway in, leaving the door open, and sat with my legs hanging out. The rain had stopped. But I knew Mike Willis would still be panicking out there in the cemetery. Even a ten-minute downpour could ruin any evidence he hadn't gotten to yet. I stared at the cemetery entrance, the uneven, bumpy track, the surrounding woodlands, and I wondered just what had happened that night. To pull off two killings in the dim light of a half-moon, even with a scope, was quite an achievement. As I watched, the new photographer, Aubrey Pugh, hurried out of the woods, through the long grass, onto the track and ran to a small, aging sedan—a Dodge Neon—and ducked inside.

"All good?" I asked as Corbin stepped up and put one hand on the top of my SUV. He nodded, tapping his empty coffee cup absently against his leg.

"What do you think?" he asked.

I shrugged, watching the teens' truck do a questionable U-turn and head back the way they'd come. McCarty had finally blocked off the road.

"Just curious kids, out and about. Hopefully, they didn't catch on to what's going on here."

Corbin nodded slowly, his gaze far away, and Samson emitted a low growl. *What was up with these two today? So anxious, especially Sam.*

But I have to admit, I was feeling it too. Two murders... like this... long-range killing of two teens out in a remote cemetery. Who does that, and why? Who takes a high-powered rifle out at night and cold-bloodedly shoots two youngsters? It was planned, premeditated. Of that, I was sure. But what could be the motive?

"See you at the office?" Corbin asked, breaking into my thoughts and turning to go to his own vehicle. "I already texted Anne and asked her to get everyone together."

I nodded, thanked him, swung my legs into the car and closed the door. A final glance at the trees shielding the cemetery from view sent a shiver down my spine.

I pushed the starter button and blew air out through my lips and put the selector into drive, made a U-turn and drove back to the main highway, again thinking about the crime scene: the grieving husband who'd found the bodies, the young girl slumped over in the passenger seat of the pickup, the blood splatter, the kid in the truck bed with half his neck blown away... *Geez! Where the hell do I begin?*

5

Saturday morning, 11 a.m.

EVEN ON THE SECOND FLOOR OF THE BUILDING, THE sound of the rain pounding down outside my office window was almost deafening. It had started back up with a vengeance on the drive back from the cemetery to the PD.

"Thanks for coming in, everyone," I said, pushing the box of pastries I'd picked up on the way back to the center of the table. I watched the team settle in and get ready to crack down.

"I hate to have to spoil your weekend," I continued, "but we have a long road ahead of us."

Anne Robar delicately picked up a croissant and began to tear it apart with her fingers. Hawk grabbed his customary strawberry frosted donut. Cooper reached over and helped himself to a cinnamon roll and shot Dani a look.

Hmm. I'll need to pay attention to that, I thought.

Danielle "Dani" Bowen was twenty-seven, a rookie detective I knew quite well since she watched Sammy whenever I had to leave him at the office, which wasn't often, usually when I had to visit someone's home. She was about five-seven with dark hair, brown eyes and an oval face—not pretty, but attractive.

Dani loved Sam, and he loved her back. It put her in my good graces, and I'd been keeping an eye on her. Hawk was supposed to be retiring soon, and if he did, I was going to need someone to step up and take his place. Meanwhile, with Tracy Ramirez on vacation, Dani was filling the gap temporarily.

She blushed slightly and shyly helped herself to a biscotti. Jack North didn't touch anything. Instead, he kicked back, sipping on a mug of black coffee.

"All right," I began, nodding to Corbin to get out his notes, "buckle in. This is a bad one and we don't have much to go on. Two youngsters were found shot to death early this morning in a cemetery. Time of death: between midnight and one-thirty in the morning. One projectile has been found and identified as a 30-30 rifle bullet. The female was shot while in the passenger side of the truck. The male was shot in the throat while trying to run, so Doc Sheddon thinks, and then picked up and placed in the truck bed."

Cooper hissed in through his teeth and a mouth full of pastry and slowly shook his head.

"That's... really bad," Anne murmured, shaking her

head. She had two boys of her own, and Hawk, her partner, had two girls. They both looked grim.

"Any witnesses?" Dani asked, still a little timid as she smoothed one side of her hair back behind her ear.

"To the murders, no," Corbin said. "All we have is the guy who found the bodies. Jeff Harper. In his early thirties. Seems straight enough. He was at the cemetery visiting his wife's grave."

"He mentioned calling a groundskeeper," I said, shifting forward in my chair. "Dani, Cooper. You two reach out to him. Corbin has his info."

Corbin nodded, consulted his notebook, wrote something on a scratch pad and handed it to Dani.

She nodded, read it, and said, "Brad Herbert?"

"Yes," Corbin replied. "That's the name and number Harper gave me. Herbert's the cemetery groundskeeper."

Cooper leaned toward his temporary partner and looked over her shoulder at the note, his eyes flickering up at her. He nodded and leaned back again.

There was a light knock on the door and Corbin stepped out to talk to an officer I recognized, but who's name I couldn't remember. I continued to describe the scene.

"I know that cemetery," Dani said suddenly, eyes widening. "Sorry... I just... You're describing that place out on Jagger Lane, right? It's not far from Booker T. Washington State Park."

I nodded, a little surprised she was familiar with the area. But then, Dani had grown up in Chattanooga and I made a note to pick her brain later about why kids would be out that way, alone.

"Hey," Corbin said as he stepped back into the room and closed the door, "we have IDs for both victims. Mike Willis found driver's licenses at the scene. Caroline Davis and Jared Moore, both seventeen. Caroline's license was tossed out into the woods—no prints. Jared's was tossed among the gravestones at the far end of the cemetery. Again, no prints."

"That's good," I said. "Now we have something to work with. Pity there were no prints, but that's to be expected. Is Doc doing the autopsies today?" I looked at Corbin.

He nodded and looked at his watch. "He said he was going to do the girl right away, and if I know him, he's already started. You want me to go observe?"

"Yes, why don't you do that," I replied.

Sergeant Corbin Russell was a few years younger than me. He'd been my partner since the chief had promoted Janet Toliver to lieutenant and reassigned her. He'd been a good choice, though at first I didn't think it was going to work. But it did, and he'd become almost an extra right hand, taking on responsibilities like attending autopsies, which I hated, and providing me with time to think. It was a good balance.

Corbin looked again at his watch and said, "I'd better go then. I'll check in with you later."

I nodded.

"So, what's the next step?" Hawk asked, shifting in

his chair and reaching under the table. I could hear Samson snorting around and figured he was harassing him for affection.

I thought for a minute, then said, "Hawk, Anne, I need you to go notify the parents. Coop, you and—"

"Canvassing, right?" Cooper asked.

Dani was eyeing him with trepidation. I tried to suppress a grin.

"Yes," I replied. "It's a pretty rural neighborhood. We ran into a couple of... I was going to call them kids, but they were hardly that. Anyway, they said they live nearby and they were curious. Their names are Ben Whitt and Luke Webber. Go and make inquiries. See what you can come up with. Talk to the local gas stations, convenience stores and be sure to check with Jeff Harper. He owns Harper's Auto shop. That truck Whitt was driving was heavily customized. Chances are he'll know them. And remember to talk to Brad Herbert, the groundskeeper. Take Dani with you."

"Right," Cooper said, closing his notebook and glancing sideways at Dani. She looked a little uncomfortable, and I sympathized. This was her first assignment as detective, but she was going to have to learn to deal with it, and quickly.

"Jack?" I said. "I need you to run backgrounds on Whitt, Webber, Brad Herbert, our two victims, and Jeff Harper; criminal, credit and especially social."

North nodded, leaning back to toss his empty cup into the bin. "On it."

The trio stood up, filing out of the room and heading for their desks. The rain sounded quieter, but it was still coming down in buckets.

Anne also stood and began tidying up the table, chasing crumbs into the mostly empty pastry box, when there was another knock at the door and a uniformed officer ducked his head in.

"Captain, there are some people here I think you'll want to see, a Cindy and Matthew Davis and their daughter Sarah."

I stood up. Anne and Hawk looked at me. They seemed as surprised as I was.

I sighed, told Sam to go to his bed under the window, then joined Hawk and Anne at the door.

"The family?" I asked, assuming the officer had already made the connection. He nodded as we headed out into the situation room and I closed my office door.

"Yes, I think so. They're wanting to speak to someone, and I thought it should go right to you."

"Good call," I said.

Something wasn't adding up. Willis had only just provided us with the victims' IDs. There was no way the families could know, not yet.

"Wait," I said and held up a hand, stopping them. "I want to make a quick stop at the computer lab and see if Jack can pull the records for Jared Moore. We need to get on top of this. If these two victims were a couple, the Davis family will be quick to call his parents, if they've not already done so."

I asked the officer to take them to one of the two conference rooms and stay with them until we got there, and we went to find Jack.

Jack had barely gotten seated when we arrived at the lab, but it didn't take him but a few seconds to pull Jared Moore's sheet. It turned out his family were foster parents, Greg and Amy Michaels. A quick scan of his record didn't show much; he'd been in the system since he was five and had been with the Michaels for five years. It seemed he'd settled in.

But there were a couple of red flags, nothing serious, during his first year with the Michaels when he was twelve.

Trespassing on school grounds after hours. Vandalism. Not uncommon for a foster kid. Jared was just a scared kid acting out. It happens all the time. Most of them get over it. Some fall through the cracks, but not this kid, so it seemed.

"We've got this," Hawk said, reaching out to take the printout from me. "We'll head over to the home right now and talk to them."

"Wait..." I said. I'd noticed a short addition at the bottom of the sheet. Jared had been caught trespassing again just four months ago.

"It looks like he hadn't grown out of his old habits," I said, pointing it out.

Anne's face fell. She bit her bottom lip and shook her head.

I handed the sheet to Hawk. He nodded, looked at

Anne and said, "Let's go." And they turned and walked away, Hawk's hulking figure overshadowing Anne, her silvery-gray hair still darkened from the rain.

"Well," I muttered as I watched them go. "I guess that leaves the Davises to me."

6

Saturday afternoon, 1 p.m.

I WENT BACK TO MY OFFICE TO CHECK ON SAMSON before heading to the conference room to interview the Davises.

"What do you think of all this, boy?" I said, turning a chair so I could sit down in front of him and gather my thoughts.

He tilted his head, wrinkled his forehead, and seemed to shrug. Okay, so I probably imagined that. He was just a dog, but a smart one.

"What could those two kids have done that someone would have wanted to kill them that way?" I asked.

Sam opened his mouth, flopped out his tongue and panted.

I looked at him and smiled, reached out and ruffled his ears. He panted harder and snapped his jaws.

"I gotta go," I said. "You be a good boy, okay? I won't

be long."

He dropped his head down between his front paws and stared up at me.

I would have loved to have stayed there with him. I had so much to think about, so many questions revolving around inside my head, but the Davises were waiting for me. *Maybe they can give me some answers.*

I stood up, reached down and patted him absently on the head, then turned and headed to the conference room and the Davis family, but I didn't enter right away.

The officer I'd asked to stay with them had stationed himself outside the door, hands clasped behind his back, frowning. The funny thing about that was that he wasn't even a part of this investigation, but he obviously thought something was off, too. That was good to know. I checked his tag. His name was E. Duncan.

"What's on your mind, Duncan?" I asked quietly. "I don't think it's a coincidence that our victim's family showed up here when they did."

He tipped his head back and forth, thinking. "The younger girl, I think she's the sister, was talking about not getting a text back. She sounded pretty upset, but it seems like the parents are trying to stay level-headed."

I nodded, feeling grim. They were doing what all parents did: they were in denial. But *I* knew their daughter's body was just three blocks away in Doc's little shop of horrors, in a cold, sanitized room, with Corbin as a witness to its ultimate violation.

"Thanks," I said as I pushed the door open and stepped inside.

They were seated together on the far side of the table flanked by three large windows.

I sat down opposite them, making a show of organizing my notebook and iPad while discreetly observing them.

What struck me was the uncanny resemblance between the victim, Caroline, and the young girl sitting across from me. They shared the same golden blonde hair and facial features. Sarah—I figured her to be about fifteen—was visibly upset. Her arms were crossed over her chest, and she kept sneaking moody glances at her parents.

"Good afternoon," I said, smiling at them. "I'm Captain Gazzara—"

"Is it our daughter, the girl who's been shot?" Mrs. Davis asked abruptly. Her face was pale, her brow furrowed, her eyes wide. "Is it Caroline? We haven't heard from her since last night."

As if on cue, Sarah Davis tapped the screen of the cell phone in front of her on the table. It lit up briefly, and a quick glance at it told me that there were no new notifications. Sarah's disappointment was plain to see.

"Mrs. Davis, Mr. Davis," I said and took a slow, deep breath. This was by far the worst part of the job. And this situation was particularly difficult. We had little to no information aside from the names of the victims. There was nothing I could tell them and, to be truthful, I was a little lost for words.

I looked up at the windows while I gathered my thoughts. The storm was still raging outside.

"How did you know about the shooting?" I asked.

"It was on the news," Mr. Davis answered, his voice oddly flat. When I'd entered the room, he'd seemed okay. Not cheerful, but not particularly upset. Unfortunately, my somewhat slow response to his wife's questions seemed to have tipped him off that something was wrong.

"The two kids they found at the cemetery," he said slowly. "Who are they?"

I pursed my lips and stared at him. We'd specifically asked the media not to release the story until... Damn it. I looked at my watch. It was already well past one o'clock in the afternoon. I'd lost track of time. We'd barely begun.

"Yes," I replied, bracing myself. "We did find two teenage victims at the cemetery on Jagger Lane. And I'm sorry to have to tell you that, yes, we believe one of them was Caroline. We have her driver's license."

Mrs. Davis broke down immediately, sobbing into her hands. Sarah's face went deathly pale, her eyes wide, fingers clutching the cell phone so tightly her knuckles were white. Mr. Davis froze, his mouth open as he looked at me in disbelief.

"We will, of course, need you to formally identify her. But I'm afraid that will have to wait. She's with the medical examiner. I'll have to check to see when he'll be ready for you. If you'll give me a minute..."

I stood up.

Mrs. Davis moaned, rocking back and forth.

Mr. Davis nodded and swallowed. "You're sure?" he asked, looking up at me. The look on my face must've told him everything he needed to know. He didn't press further, so I went to the door and opened it. Duncan was still stationed outside.

"Hey," I said, closing the door behind me so they wouldn't hear. "Do me a favor. Call Doc Sheddon's office and find out when he'll be done with Caroline Davis. Tell them I have her parents here and they've agreed to identify the body. Then come and let me know, okay?"

"Yes, ma'am." And he turned and hurried away.

Me? I took a deep breath and returned to my seat.

"Mr. and Mrs. Davis, Sarah. I'm so sorry for your loss. I've sent someone to find out when you can see the... Caroline." I hastily corrected myself, but they didn't seem to notice. "But I have to ask you; aside from what you heard on the news, what brought you here? What made you think Caroline might be involved?"

Mrs. Davis shot her youngest daughter a look bordering on cruel. I'd seen it happen many times when emotional barriers broke down. Sarah, however she was involved, would remember that look for the rest of her life.

"Tell her," the woman demanded.

Sarah's voice was thick with grief when she spoke, unable to meet my eyes. "I... I covered for her. Last night. She was sneaking out—"

"To see that boy," Mr. Davis broke in. His words filled with anger. "Was he involved somehow? Did he kill her? Jared something... Shit! What's his last name?"

"Howard, your language," Mrs. Davis choked out. "Jared Moore. Did he—"

"I'm sorry," I interrupted firmly. "I can't provide

details, but I can tell you in good faith that Jared is not involved the way you're thinking. And no, he didn't kill her. Sarah, you said you covered for her. Was this the first time?"

Sarah shook her head, at first slowly, then more vigorously. "No." She glanced at her parents. Sometimes it was hard to get info out of kids with their parents in the room, but if Mr. and Mrs. Davis left, we'd have to go through a rollercoaster of paperwork to get their consent to speak with her. Better that they stay. For now.

"Go on," I said.

"No," she continued. "Caroline tried to see Jared once a week. At least. They've been dating for a while."

Mr. Davis was shaking his head. "I told her not to go near that boy."

"You don't like him," I said. "Why's that?"

Did they know anything about what I'd read just moments ago in his file? If so, I wasn't surprised by the way they felt. No kid is ever good enough, no matter their reputation, especially one who was known to break the rules, as Jared was.

The man scowled, his eyes red-rimmed. "Jared's a troublemaker. He's gotten into fights at the school, and..."

As Mr. Davis continued to list the strikes against the deceased teen, I snuck a glance at Sarah. She looked guilty. If I had to guess, she'd probably been the one to tell her parents about Jared's behavior. Maybe it started as excitement, gossiping about the school "bad boy," only for the tide to turn when Caroline took an interest in him.

Davis didn't mention any of what I'd seen on the

boy's file, though.

"And from whom did you hear all this?" I asked.

Mrs. Davis wiped her eyes and said, "Shouldn't you check with the school about that? We just... We've heard about these things. Parents talk, you know."

My bullshit meter was going off, but I didn't feel like pushing them. They were already on the defensive. Instead, I turned back to Sarah.

"Sarah, tell me about last night."

The girl nodded, sniffing loudly. "I... I watched her sneak out," she admitted guiltily, subconsciously leaning away from her parents. "Jared parks a few houses down. Caroline climbs out the window and goes to his truck."

Mrs. Davis was rigid with anger. The need to defend the youngster was palpable, but I reeled it in and focused on Sarah; but before she could speak, Mr. Davis broke in.

"You should look into Chase, too. I bet he had something to do with this." His face had turned a darker shade of red, his anger spilling over as he continued to rant.

I held up a hand and stopped him. "Hold on. I'm sorry. Who's Chase?"

"He's Jared's brother," Mrs. Davis said bitterly. "The two of them were always running around town, causing trouble. I heard they broke a bunch of windows in that new development at Deer Run Acres. I heard..."

I tuned her out and made a note in my pad, "Chase Moore?"

"No, it's Richards," Sarah whispered, obviously watching what I was writing. We all looked at her; she'd sunk into her seat and was crying silently.

"He has a different last name than Jared," she said quietly. "He was a senior a few years ago."

I crossed out Moore and added the name Richards, promising myself I'd have him checked out as soon as I left the room. But there were still a few questions left unanswered... questions that were itching at the base of my skull.

"Did Caroline have any enemies? Do you know of anyone that might have wanted to hurt her? Anyone she'd fallen out with lately?" I said, noting the outrage on Mrs. Davis' face.

The parents, of course, confirmed that Caroline was a sweet girl, innocent, just caught up with the wrong boy, blah blah. I'd heard it all a thousand times before. And judging from my own short experience with the Davises, I could understand why Caroline wanted to sneak out and ride around town with a cute boy. That also happens all the time. And it wasn't always a bad thing. Far from it. But...

"And Jared, Sarah? Can you think of anyone *specifically* who would want to hurt him? Just tell me what you know, personally."

I didn't want to hear any more gossip about Jared, just facts.

Mr. Davis seemed to understand that, and he interrupted his wife as she opened her mouth to speak, "Jared Moore had plenty of enemies, I'm sure, but I don't know of any in particular. Sarah?"

Sarah shook her head slowly, her brow furrowed. She caught on quicker than her parents.

"Wait. If Caroline's... dead," she said and choked on the word, "does that mean Jared is too?"

A quick glance at the clock told me that by now, Hawk and Anne were with Jared's family and they'd been notified.

I nodded and said, "Please understand that what I tell you must stay in this room. You can't; you must not talk to anyone, especially the press. If we're to find whoever did this to your daughter, we need to keep the details of the investigation under wraps. But yes, Jared Moore was also killed. They were together in his truck. In the cemetery on Jagger Lane. Do you have any idea what they might have been doing there?" *Apart from the obvious,* I thought dryly.

I already knew, from seeing a copy of Caroline's driver's license, that they lived some six miles from the cemetery.

I looked back and forth at the trio. Mrs. Davis' gaze was glassy. Mr. Davis' face was completely drained of color; he looked like a corpse come to life. Sarah continued to cry quietly.

"No," Mr. Davis finally answered. "No, I... Caroline never mentioned the cemetery."

From the look on his face, it was clear that *his* role in this was finally coming to realization. By forbidding his daughter to see Jared Moore and being so hateful toward the teen boy, he'd only pushed her into his arms. Into the truck where she'd died.

"How about a Ben Whitt and Luke Webber?" I asked. "D'you know anything about them?"

I was answered by three blank looks, then Mr. Davis said, "No, but why d'you want to know? Are they suspects?"

"No!" I snapped. "Absolutely not. They turned up at the cemetery during the preliminary investigation of the crime scene, a couple of spectators on their way somewhere else."

Taking a deep breath, I gave the family a moment to compose themselves before I asked my next question. Something seemingly absurd that had been weighing on my mind. But also something that we'd been seeing more of over the last year. In fact, we had two officers, detectives, assigned especially to it. And the attack had, after all, taken place in a cemetery, at night.

"Mr. and Mrs. Davis, Sarah. Did Caroline ever express an interest in witchcraft, or the occult, maybe? Have you ever heard anything about cult activities in the area?"

Everyone looked at me in total amazement, shaking their heads.

"Witchcraft? The occult?" Mr. Davis spit out. "Are you serious, Captain? No, of course not. Why would you ask such a question? I've never heard of anything like that going on around here." His eyes met mine and locked on. "All I can tell you is that you should track down Chase Richards and ask him what happened to our daughter. If anyone knows, he does."

It was at that moment that Duncan knocked on the door. I went and opened it.

"After six this evening," he said.

7

Saturday afternoon, 2:45 p.m.

CORBIN HAD REAPPEARED A LITTLE AFTER TWO-thirty that afternoon and found Samson and me alone in my office staring up at the whiteboard which, except for five names, was blank: those of the two victims, Chase Richards, Ben Whitt and Luke Webber. He came in carrying two cups of tea. The steam smelled of bergamot and lavender. A calming combination, although it didn't do much to take the edge off of my increasingly somber mood. *Maybe a nice glass of red instead...*

"That bad?" Corbin asked, wiping his top lip, where the sheen of Vicks VapoRub still lingered.

"Not really," I replied. "I met with the girl's parents and younger sister. Not an easy interview, but then, they never are, are they? Nothing really helpful, except for a name." I nodded at the white board, made a face, leaned back in my chair and ruffled Samson's ears; he was lying at my side, behind my desk. "They didn't like Jared, not at all. Said he was a troublemaker. They also mentioned that he had a brother, Chase Richards... I'd say he was adopted too."

I glanced up at the clock on the wall.

"Anne and Hawk should be back from the Michaels' any time now. Caroline's parents obviously had a beef with Jared, but I don't think they knew how often she was seeing him. Seems like Jared was something of a badass, liked to fight. Same with his brother."

"Something's bothering you," Corbin said, smiling at me. I gifted him with a tired smile, shook my head and sighed.

Samson whined, stood up and put his heavy head in my lap. I kneaded his ear with one hand as I thought, frowning.

"It's just that... I don't think it was personal," I said. "They were shot from a distance. I mean, like the killer was a sniper, and after midnight, in the dark, well, semi-dark. Who does that? It's weird, right?"

Corbin nodded, his own lips flat and tight. "Yeah. Doc pointed that out, too. He said shooting isn't usually a personal crime. There's no passion to it. And especially at a distance... it took time. Patience. It couldn't have been random. I mean, like you said. Who does that?"

I drummed my fingers on the desk. Sammy whined again. "It's okay, boy," I murmured.

I glanced up at the clock again. "I need something to eat. We should grab lunch before Anne and Hawk get back."

Corbin nodded and stood, wiping his top lip again. He was at the door when my phone rang. I motioned him on, watching as he shut the door quietly behind him with a click.

"Gazzara," I answered the call.

"Hey, Kate. It's Mike Willis."

Samson sat down hard at my side.

"Hey," I said in surprise. "This is early to be hearing from you."

He grunted. "Well, with the storm, we couldn't really stay out there long."

I frowned. He sounded flustered. *Really* flustered. Willis was a meticulous CSI tech, combing over every inch of a crime scene relentlessly. He'd given me the consequential lead more times than I could count, and to think that he, too, was operating at a loss made me nervous.

"I have a report for you, but it's short," he said. "There's just not much to work with." He sighed.

This wasn't good.

"Honestly, Kate, there wasn't much out there," he continued. "It was cleaner than most of the scenes I've processed, and that makes me nervous. A wild place like that... I was expecting more, much more. But I can tell you more about what the squirrels were getting up to than I can about the killer."

He recited an incredibly short list of things we already knew: the bullet caliber; the type of gun we should be looking for; that every item in the immediate area, aside from Jeff Harper's flowers, belonged to no one but the victims.

"Kate, it reminds me a little too much of those teen slasher movies that used to come out in the eighties," he said, dating himself. "You know, teens getting picked off in the woods while they were hooking up. Like some trigger-happy psycho is out there waiting for them. And whoever it was, knew what they were doing, because we searched the woods too and didn't find a damn thing. We did find an area where he might have been standing; the grass was flattened. Maybe Ballistics will be able to give us the make and model of rifle."

"I'm sorry, Mike," I said. "And I'm right there with you. But listen, I know you did all you could, and with this storm, I'm surprised you found anything at all. The wallets—they were most helpful, and to find them in that long grass in this weather. You guys did great. Thank you."

He muttered a few choice words about the storm, which was still raging outside, and then said, "Right. Well, I'll leave you to it, Kate, but I'm here if anything else comes up. Just let me know."

I promised and hung up, then leaned back in my chair. I sat there for a moment thinking. I couldn't get the idea of a sniper out of my mind. *It had to be random. There's no other scenario that makes sense, not that I can think of.*

I received a text from Anne letting me know that they'd be back in the building in ten minutes. Figuring there was no point in lunch, I sat down at my desk and decided to pull up Chase Richards' file.

The first thing I was curious about was their mismatched surnames. And, just as I'd thought, they were half-brothers. I stared at the photo of Chase that came up in the database. In my mind, it was almost a mirror image of the teen in the truck bed, eyes glazed and staring blankly at the sky. I printed it and taped it up on the whiteboard.

Chase Richards had darker hair than Jared, but they shared the same nose. He was nineteen and had just aged out of the foster care system and lived on his own. *Free to wreak havoc on the community,* I thought, scrolling down, giving a low whistle at the length of his rap sheet.

Everything from petty theft to assault to possession, even a DUI last summer. Everything *but* murder. I carefully clicked on and read through each report, taking notes as I did so, focusing on the assaults.

And the pieces started to come together for me. I printed the report and spread the pages out on my desk.

Chase Richards wasn't a killer. Every one of his assaults had taken place in a bar. He had a drinking problem, that was clear, which meant he probably shouldn't be working the lumber yard job his parole officer had listed as a current place of employment.

"Too bad," I murmured to myself as my suspicions melted away into pity. Too often we saw these foster kids age out and, because of what they'd had to deal with in the system and the urge to forget, they often ended up deep into drugs or alcohol or both. It wouldn't have surprised me if Chase Richards found himself in prison soon, with or without a murder charge.

But could a brother kill his sibling? I wondered. It was possible. It wasn't unknown...

I stood, grabbing my things and texting Anne back to report to Corbin when she got here.

"Come on, boy," I said, wrapping Sammy's leash around my wrist. "We have work to do."

Regardless of his run-ins with the law, Chase deserved to hear about his brother's death directly, not from the news media that would, I was sure, soon be releasing the victims' names. Plus, I wanted to see how bad of an ass Chase Richards really was, and the best way to do that was to talk to him face-to-face.

8

Saturday afternoon, 3:15 p.m.

LYON & HOLMES LUMBER WAS IN THE MIDDLE OF A
shift change, and when I pulled in, a half-dozen trucks
were pulling out of the muddy yard. I ignored the curious
stares of the workers as they trundled past my SUV, but
Sammy was on high alert, his ears pricked forward as he
stood on the center console.

"Back, boy," I told him quietly.

By three that afternoon it had quit raining, but the
yard was a mess. The open space surrounding the warehouse was unpaved, a minefield of muddy tracks where
every little dip was filled with water. My tires splashed
through as I pulled up to the converted storage container
that served as the office. At first glance it appeared there
was no one inside. The activity seemed to be centered on
the giant double sliding doors that gave entrance to the

warehouse, where an eclectic group of people were standing around, smoking and chatting.

I parked as close to the doors as I could, trying to find a dry spot; there was no designated parking lot. I opened the back door and let Sammy out, keeping him at a close heel. He trotted at my side, splashing mud up my pants, but so be it.

"Hey," I called to the nearest worker, a lean young guy smoking a crinkled cigarette. He half-turned, looked me over and nodded. As I approached, I realized that despite his youth, his face was a landscape of wrinkles and scars. He was also missing half of his left forefinger.

"Where can I find Chase Richards?" I asked.

The man's expression didn't change as he reached out, let Sammy sniff his hand, and ruffled the scruff of his neck. "Nice dog."

"Thanks... so, Chase Richards?"

His glance was quick, but I caught the mistrust in it. He looked toward the large building and tipped his head. "Would probably be in there. You'll need a hard hat. You'll find some on a rack just inside the doors."

I stepped away awkwardly, picking my way through the mud into the building where, sure enough, a dozen or so hard hats were hanging on a rack just to the right. I grabbed one and put it on.

The noise inside the building was beyond loud, but Samson didn't so much as flinch. He stood at my side as I looked around. The howl of the giant circular saw ripping a huge tree trunk into planks was ear-shattering, drowning out the sound of men and women shouting to one another. None of them were wearing ear protection. The air was misty with sawdust, causing me to cough, and I had to wonder what the EPA would make of it. None of the workers seemed bothered by it, though.

In fact, they seemed more bothered at the sight of me than the noise and the sawdust. I walked further into the building. For the most part, I was ignored. A couple of people nodded to me, but most of them just turned their backs. I figured it was the badge hanging from a chain around my neck. Inwardly, I had to smile as I recognized some of them. In fact, over the course of my career, I must have come across at least twenty-five percent of the more than sixty individuals working there. A lumber yard is a tough place to work and requires tough people to run it. This one was no exception.

I stopped, looked around, then glanced down at Samson. He seemed calm enough, close by my side, sitting on his haunches, his ears pricked—a good sign.

"Chase Richards?" I asked a young woman nearby. Her mouth twisted into a half snarl as she looked at me, but she pointed to an area at the back of the building and to the right.

I nodded and thanked her, but she just turned away, still without saying a word. I shrugged it off and walked carefully, almost the full length of the building, to an area where the raw wood was stored.

It was much quieter back there; the noise of the saws was muted, and the rear doors were wide open. A chill breeze wafted through the building, clearing the air of sawdust. A truck loaded with tree trunks parked outside, its wheels sunk into the mud.

Again, I approached one of the workers and asked where I could find Chase. He bent his head in my direction and pointed to a man working a forklift.

I nodded my thanks and headed in that direction. As I approached, I recognized the dark hair curling under the hard hat.

"Hey!" I shouted.

Chase turned to look at me, and I was surprised to see how clean and tidy he was. His skin was clear, even pretty, and his eyes were a striking blue.

"Chase Richards?" I asked, already knowing the answer, having recognized him from his file photo, which had obviously been taken only a few months earlier.

Chase turned off the lift and climbed down, smirking, and leaned against the forklift as he looked me up and down.

Samson, not reading the room apparently, panted happily and walked up to him, sniffed his leg, then looked up at him and wagged his tail. Chase looked down at him warily but didn't try to pet him or move away. *Hmm. Interesting.*

"Who's asking?" he finally said, blue eyes flitting from my badge back to mine.

I'm sure it wasn't the first time a cop had come looking for him at his place of work, but he didn't seem too bothered. I dug my badge out anyway. "Captain Gazzara. Chattanooga police. We need to talk."

I always hated breaking the news of a death to a

family member, but the thought of doing it there, in that industrial warehouse, didn't sit well with me. Without even looking, I could feel his co-workers watching.

Chase smirked and, casually taking a cigarette out of his shirt pocket, said, "Sorry. Can't leave my station. If I do, the boss'll be pissed. How can I help you?"

Despite his young age, he came across as surprisingly mature. He didn't have the lean, lanky body of an adolescent, either, but I figured if he'd been working at the lumber yard for any length of time, that would explain the muscled body and arms.

Chase Richards exuded a confidence that I hadn't been expecting. *How long has this kid been relying only on himself?* I wondered. Knowing the system as I did, I figured it was probably from an early age.

Samson was, by then, sitting happily *on* Chase's work boot, looking up at me, his tongue lolling out, and that made me feel a whole lot better about the boy. The Davis family might have had a bad feeling about him, but if Samson trusted him, then so did I. Not that I'd ever admit anything like that to the chief; he'd have a conniption fit if he knew I was operating not only on my gut instinct but my dog's as well.

"It's about your brother, Jared," I said as he lit up unapologetically, indoors, in all that sawdust. A lit match or lighter was an explosion waiting to happen. "And I really think we should take that outside."

Chase's face darkened. He frowned. His eyes narrowed. I knew what he was thinking. Jared was in trouble again?

"Have you called his foster parents?" he asked, pushing himself off the lift, startling Samson, who leaped away, then turned, wagging his tail.

The kid turned his back on me and walked away toward the back entrance. I followed him. He stopped just inside the door and flicked the cigarette out through the open door into the mud. I looked at it floating in a puddle of dirty water and noticed that it had begun to drizzle again. *Oh that's just great.*

"Chase, I'm sorry, but there's no easy way to tell you this. We found your brother early this morning. He's dead."

Chase Richards didn't react... at all.

I stood there watching him, waiting for a reaction, something. But all I got was a stare and stony silence. The cigarette's smoke curled up into the drizzle.

"I already know," he said finally, shifting his weight from one foot to the other. He lowered his head and stared down at his boots, his hands deep in his pockets. "Greg called me earlier. Didn't bother to show up in person, like you did, so... thanks." His voice was almost devoid of emotion, but I picked up a hint of bitterness.

Greg and Amy Michaels! Jared's foster parents. I wonder if he's on good terms with them.

Inwardly, I sighed. *This could have been handled better!* I thought, but I knew either Anne or Hawk would've told me if there'd been any indication the Michaels would call Chase. No. It had been unavoidable.

"I'm sorry, Chase," I said. "You deserved better...

Chase, was your brother happy with his foster family? Did they get along?"

Chase's eyebrows knitted, shadowed by the lip of the hard hat. "Why d'you ask?" he replied. "Greg said he was shot. Do you think he did himself in or something?"

And there it was, the anger in his voice. I shook my head. "No. Jared didn't shoot himself. Did he have any enemies? D'you know of anyone who might have had a grudge against him? Anyone he might have offended? Was he into drugs? Anything?"

Chase snorted. "Oh, Jared had issues, all right. We both did." He admitted it without reservation. The kid was surprisingly self-aware, especially considering his background.

"I aged out of the system last year. It's been a little better for me since then." He shrugged. "Trying to break old habits, you know? The judge has me seeing a therapist. It's not too bad. But Jared... he got lucky with the Michaels. Greg might be an unfeeling son of a bitch to call and tell me like that, but they were good to Jared. He liked it there, too; so if you're asking if they had something to do with it somehow, then I'd say no. No way."

"Were you and Jared close?" I asked, but Chase was already shaking his head.

"Hadn't seen him in a minute," he said. That was a new one on me. I assumed he meant, in a while. "Sometimes I'd text him to check in, but I can't tell you much, Captain, about whatever he had going on. All I can tell you is that he never mentioned anyone coming after him or whatever; not to me, he didn't."

I frowned. What Chase was telling me, his reactions, and his answers weren't what I'd been expecting. Even so, I had a gut feeling that he had nothing to do with his brother's death. I needed more.

"Was it your choice, or his, to keep your distance?" I asked.

Chase shrugged. "Mine, I guess." He stared into my eyes for a moment, catching on that I wasn't making the connection. He smiled and said, "Captain, I know how you guys work. I know you've already looked me up. You saw my rap sheet. Like I said, Jared got lucky with the Michaels. He's been with them a while, and I wanted him to have a decent chance. A better chance than I did, you know?"

Looking down, the kid sniffed and wiped at his nose with the back of his hand. He tried to disguise it, but I could see the glint of emotion in his eyes. It must have hurt terribly, having to keep his distance from his brother in order to give him a better shot at life, only for Jared to...

If I sat down with Chase Richards and asked him for his backstory, I wondered, *what would I hear that wasn't included in those files? What kind of sick things had he had to deal with while in foster care that forced him to act out the way he did? What was it that turned a nineteen-year-old kid into a grown man before his time?* I really would have liked to have known.

But everything about the conversation was telling me that Chase Richards didn't have anything to do with Jared and Caroline's deaths. I whistled, calling Sammy, who had wandered off toward a logging truck, back to my side.

Now that he'd had a minute to gather himself, Chase asked me, "Greg said there was someone else with him, with Jared."

"Yes. A girl. We think they were dating. Caroline Davis."

He nodded. "Sounds familiar, yeah." And then Chase looked at me sharply, squinting. "Now that I think about it," he said, digging in his pocket for another cigarette, "I remember Jared mentioning something about her."

My ears perked up. "Oh? What was that?"

"Yeah, he told me he was into her, but *she* was into some weird stuff," he said as he lit up and blew out a huge cloud of smoke.

Oh, great. The last thing I needed to hear about was whatever sex life these kids had gotten up to.

Chase, apparently reading my mind, grinned and said, "No! Nothing like that. Just witchy stuff, I guess. When they first met, he wasn't so sure he wanted to keep on dating her because she was into magic or something."

I frowned. This whole time something in the back of my mind had been chanting *cult, cult, cult*, but what were the chances of that actually happening? After all, as Willis had said, that was the kind of thing you saw in slasher films. Not real life.

"How did Jared know she was into that kind of thing?" I asked, taking out my notepad and a ballpoint.

Chase continued to squint, staring off into the

distance as he tried to recall. "He said she was hanging out with this chick named Jasmine. If that's true, then, yeah, Caroline was probably into that stuff, 'cause she definitely is."

"What makes you say that?"

Chase chuckled darkly. "Jasmine? I can't remember her last name. We went to school together. We didn't run in the same circles, but she stood out. In a bad way. She was into some really weird stuff. Dead animals. I remember some kids said they found her messing with a dead cat on the side of the road."

I made a note: Jasmine? Witchcraft? My mind was whirling. *Witchcraft? Really?* But the thought of someone messing around with dead animals... Kids were known to experiment with all kinds of weird stuff, but it never lasted long. Well, most times. But dead animals? That was one of the indicators of a future serial killer and other kinds of twisted predilections, so I didn't want to rule it out.

"You're sure you don't remember her last name?" I asked.

He shook his head.

"But you and Jared went to the same school, right?"

He nodded.

It wouldn't be difficult to find out who Jasmine was. I'd have someone on my team reach out to the school.

He took another big hit off the cigarette, looked around conspiratorially, and said, "Listen, I don't want to create no trouble with this. I don't know for a fact that Jasmine is involved. It's just a guess."

I nodded. "Don't worry. We'll do the research. Chase, is there anything I can do for you?"

I trailed off, feeling the need to make the offer but having no idea how I could help him. He was a few months away from his last incident, in therapy, working a full-time job. All I could really do was hope that he'd found his way out of the cycle of failure the system created.

He shook his head, dropped the cigarette, and stamped it out. "Just find who killed my brother," he said flatly. "And please give me a call when you do, Captain." His voice was hard, almost dead, and in it, I heard what I'd been missing the entire conversation: that promise of violence.

Chase Richards would allow us to do our job, but there was a part of him, a part deep inside him, that yearned for revenge. I hoped he would keep it caged.

9

Saturday afternoon, 4 p.m.

SAMMY JUMPED IN THE BACK OF THE SUV, LEAVING muddy paw marks on the seat. I looked at him and frowned. He showed his teeth, smiling at me and wagging his tail. *How the hell can I ever be mad at the mutt?*

I closed the door, went to the front and slid inside. I was about to punch the starter button when my cell vibrated.

"Hey, Chief. What's up?"

"Kate, we need to talk about this case you've caught. My office. ASAP."

Frowning, I thumbed the starter button and wondered what the hell it was about. Had he heard something and wanted to bring me up to speed? Had he caught up with a member or members of my team and persuaded them to give up what they had before reporting it to me? If he had, I'd be pissed. I liked to be up to date on everything before I bearded the lion, Johnston, in his den. A call like that was not unusual, but it never boded anything good.

"Sure," I replied. "I'm heading back now. Shouldn't be more than ten minutes."

I hung up and carefully maneuvered my almost new SUV out of the lot, which was now little more than a mud pit. It would take days for it to dry up. We hadn't seen a storm that bad since last year's hurricane season. Sammy licked his paws and whined.

He'd seemed so okay with Chase Richards. I just couldn't see the nineteen-year-old killing his brother. Yes, he had a pretty bad track record. Worse than his brother's. But nothing that pointed to murder.

Plus, I could appreciate him wanting to keep his distance from Jared and give the kid a chance. Call me a softy if you like, but there's good and bad in all of us. I figured Chase was a victim of the system and was prepared to give him the benefit of the doubt.

Samson whined again, put his chin on the back of my seat and licked my ear, making me shudder.

"It's okay, boy," I murmured. "The chief is probably just gonna tell us to get out ahead of the press." I rolled my eyes as I repeated Wesley Johnston's favorite line.

"You NEED to get out ahead of the press," Johnston said solemnly, rounding his desk. I stared straight at him, not even wanting to blink in case he could sense my sarcasm. *Shocker*.

Corbin cleared his throat and crossed his legs. I'd have bet anything he was having the same reaction as I was, but Corbin was, like me, too respectful to let on.

"Okay, so I'll call the press in and give them the minimum," I offered, though I'd already texted Anne and asked her to make the call while we were in the meeting. She and Hawk were writing up their reports, as were Jack, Dani and Cooper, and I wanted to get my hands on those last two. They'd spoken to the groundskeeper, I hoped... *What was his name?*

"Kate!"

Johnston's tone told me that he'd already said my name more than once. I snapped back to reality. "Sorry, Chief, I was just thinking."

With a sigh, the chief repeated himself. "You know the drill, Catherine. Just the basics. No more than that. Do not release the names. Omit whatever you think can help us solve this thing quickly."

Corbin was frowning. "Sorry, Chief, but I'm not sure we'll be able to do that; solve it quickly. The cemetery is pretty isolated, and we have no witnesses and precious little physical evidence. The rain—"

"Yes, yes. I know all about the rain," he snapped. "What we need here is good old-fashioned police work. Leg work. That's what it's going to take: leg work. The scene. It's out near Booker T., right?"

"Yes, sir," Corbin replied. "Not many people live

around there. Jack said they hit seven houses total in a one-mile radius."

That was pretty sparse but not surprising. Anyone living that far outside of the city wanted peace, quiet, and a good chunk of land.

Johnston sighed and sat down. "How bad is it?" he asked, his eyes locked on mine intently. "The scene? It's been pouring non-stop for almost two days. I'm told the guys in the motor pool shop are building an ark."

I smiled at his weak attempt at humor, then said, "It's pretty bad. Willis wasn't able to get much before the rain set in; but they did manage to find one of the bullets, which was a miracle in itself, along with two wallets and, as far as I know, that's it. We do know the kids were shot at long range with a 30-30, and we have a time of death: midnight to one-thirty."

"Well, all right then," Johnston said, rousing himself with an energy that made me perk up in expectation. "Here's what you're going to do. I want you to reach out to the Park Rangers' office and get them involved. They know that area well."

It was like a sucker punch to the gut. Even Corbin looked upset.

"But, Chief," I said. "This is our case and—"

"I know, I know," he snapped, "but the cemetery borders on state land. We have no jurisdiction there. So get them involved. The more resources, the better. I don't doubt you and your team, Kate, but you're going to need all the help you can get. Stop taking it personally. Think of the victims."

Taking it personally? Of course I did. That was a second punch to the gut, though perhaps it was deserved. What was coming next? Was he going to tell me to get the Tennessee Wildlife Resource Agency involved? I sure as hell hoped not.

Humbled, I settled back into my chair. The chief was right. There was no point in getting my feelings hurt over it. We had no real suspects—not even persons of interest. Not only that, my team and I had more than enough on our plates with other cases. And, in less than an hour, I'd have to deal with the press. And from there... Well, I had no idea. And my mind began to wander again.

I remembered the name Chase Richards had given me: Jasmine. I didn't particularly want to open up the occult can of worms, but I figured I'd be doing Caroline and Jared a disservice by writing it off as silly rumors. I glanced at Corbin, knowing I had to catch him up on this as soon as we set foot outside of the chief's office.

"Anything else, Chief?" Corbin asked. It was obvious from his posture that he was gearing up for our press conference, too, and probably not excited about it.

Johnston scowled. "Just the usual. Keep at it, and keep digging. The community always gets worked up when kids are the victims. The faster we get this thing solved, the better."

We both nodded and then excused ourselves.

Once outside, I checked my messages and saw I had a text from Anne. I was right. *Press in an hour*. I sighed.

"Just time enough to get a quick bite. You want something, Corbin? My treat. I'm going to call Peggy Sanchez over at the park ranger's office."

He frowned, and I realized that he hadn't met Peggy yet. We'd had no need to involve her in any of our cases recently.

"She's been with the state for a little more than twenty years," I said. "She's the one person I don't mind stepping on our toes."

Corbin nodded. "Sounds good, Captain. What are you going to have?"

"I'll run across the road to McDonald's," I said, feeling a little guilty since I'd eaten from there almost every day that week.

He laughed, said he'd have his usual burger and fries, and promised to get the team together while I was gone.

"Here, take Sammy for me," I said and held out the leash, ignoring the dog's forlorn expression. "Last thing I need is for him to eat something weird off the sidewalk. Thanks, Corbin."

The sky was overcast, but the rain had stopped and it was starting to dry up a little. The walk across Amnicola at that time of day was, to say the least, dangerous. Rush hour anywhere in Chattanooga is dangerous, but Amnicola?

I put in my order of three burgers—one for me, Corbin, and Sammy—and then, at the last second, I added five orders of fries for everyone to share. I figured we'd be at it for at least another couple of hours.

As I waited, I scrolled through my contacts, found

Peggy's and called her. It rang for a minute and then went to voicemail. *Damn it!*

"Hey, Peg. It's Kate Gazzara. Give me a call whenever you have a minute. It's important. Thanks."

Again, I was beaten by the time. McDonald's at four-thirty on a Saturday afternoon was busy, really busy, and I had to wait for my order. By the time I made it back across the road, it was time to meet the press. So I handed off the food to an officer, asked him to take it upstairs, then went to the restroom, where I straightened myself up. Then I stepped into the lion's den: the press room.

It went better than I expected. Corbin joined me, and together we gave them the bare essentials and then took a few questions, the answers to most of which were: "'I'm not at liberty to answer that at this time,' or, 'the investigation is ongoing.'"

By five-twenty, we were back in my office where the rest of my team was waiting, seated at the table, including Dani and Cooper, who were obviously excited about something.

10

Saturday evening, 5 p.m.

"How did it go?" Hawk asked as I sat down at the table and grabbed my now cold burger.

"Quickly," Corbin said. "Just the facts, ma'am."

"Hah. Lucky you," I heard Hawk mutter under his breath. Hawk hated press conferences. We all did. I couldn't think of any sworn officers who didn't. There was no joy in laying yourself open to the traps, tricks, quotes taken out of context, and games that many of the members of the fourth estate like to play while in search of a sensational tidbit of information. But it is what it is, and we have to put up with their machinations—and with a smile on our faces.

"So," I said between bites, looking at Cooper. "What have you two been up to?"

Dani took a deep breath. Cooper looked at her and nodded. *Interesting.*

"There's just something weird about him," she said, leaning forward.

Beneath the table, I could hear Sammy sniffing out whatever crumbs were left over from his burger.

"About who?" I asked.

"Brad... um..."

"Herbert," Cooper supplied. "He's the groundskeeper at the cemetery. Has been for the last eight years. Before that, he was employed by the city doing general maintenance. His performance reviews were so-so, but as soon as he was transferred to the cemetery job, his reviews improved."

"How so?" I asked, frowning.

"He was excited by it," Dani answered, glancing up at me. "By what happened there. At first I thought he was an addict. He was jumpy, rambling, talking fast. But he kept looking over to where the victim's truck was—before Mike Willis removed it to the pound. It was like the murders excited him."

I glanced at Cooper, who nodded. He'd been on the force long enough to have a feel for things, even if he did tend to goof off now and then. If Cooper had picked up on it, it was a red flag.

"Okay, so you think he's a death junkie, then? So what?"

"That's not all of it," Cooper said, leaning forward. "He *really* is a death junkie, Cap. He kept making all these weird references to death. How it's part of the natural process, a cycle. Then he said something about an... ouroboros?"

By the way he looked at Dani, it was obvious Cooper didn't know what that meant. He was just parroting whatever Brad Herbert had said. But the image of it appeared in my head: a serpent eating its own tail. A reference to the cycle of life, death, and rebirth. It was something I'd seen before, a long time ago.

Dani picked up where Cooper left off. "He actually said he talks to the dead, to dead people."

Now that got my attention. "I'm sorry. He said *what*?"

"He said he talks to dead people," Cooper said. "And I don't think he was joking. He was serious."

I pursed my lips, frowned, and stared at the two of them. I needed to know more. It sounded like Brad Herbert was a total nut, and it made him an addition to my *very* short list of suspects.

"Okay... I need a little more here," I said. "What exactly did he mean by 'talks to dead people'?"

"He said he can sense the presence of spirits," Cooper replied, "and that they communicate with him. He said he's an 'open channel.' While we were there, he kept telling Dani that she had a male relative who wanted to talk to her."

Dani looked at me and shrugged.

"That's just weird," Jack said. "And unbelievable. The guy's an intrusive creep."

"Reach out to Jeff Harper," I said to Cooper. "The guy who found our two victims. He said Herbert was a friend. Ask him about him. Ask if he's been in touch with his deceased wife."

"Does he have an alibi for Friday night?" Corbin asked.

Dani nodded.

"He was with a friend, Jasmine Hall. We didn't get the chance to talk to her, but—"

"Wait." I leaned forward, took out my notebook and flipped through the pages to the notes I made while talking to Chase Richards.

"Jasmine," I said. "Chase Richards, Jared Moore's brother, mentioned her. He didn't have a last name. It would make sense, though. Chase mentioned that she was into witchcraft."

"How did he know her?" Hawk asked.

"He said he went to school with her, and Jared mentioned to him that Caroline Davis was somehow involved with her."

Jack raised his eyebrows at me. I knew what he was thinking, but I didn't want to make the connection to cult activity.

"We still need to confirm the last name," I said. "Chase doesn't remember it, so I'll have to reach out to the school, and I can't do that until Monday morning. So, in the meantime, let's put her up on the whiteboard, and Herbert, too. Where did he say they were last night, by the way? How old is he?"

Dani and Cooper exchanged a look before Cooper answered, "Early thirties, I think. He said they were at her house. Apparently, she lives in town, but he didn't know the actual address."

"Now that's a crock," I said. "How can he not know the address if he was there?"

Herbert wasn't doing himself any favors.

"All right," I said impatiently. "So, we need to confirm Jasmine's last name and make sure it's the one Chase remembers. Either way, we need to question her, if only to confirm Herbert's alibi. If it's a match, we'll bring her in for questioning. The chances are slim that there are two Jasmines involved, but stranger things, right? So it's better to be safe than sorry."

It was at that moment my cell rang for what seemed like the hundredth time that day. I almost turned it over, screen down and ignored it, but I didn't. And a good thing, too. It was Chief Johnston.

"Check out the news," he said when I answered.

I looked at my watch. It was just after six.

I thanked him for the heads-up and turned on the TV on the credenza behind my desk. Samson, lounging in his bed under the office window, lifted his head and stared up at the screen.

"We have breaking news," the lead anchor said. "Two teens tragically lost their lives last night..."

There wasn't much more. Corbin and I had filled them in on the bare minimum; no details about the cause of death, time, weapon, wounds, or location. No, they hadn't been pleased, but they had to put up with it. We needed to keep the details locked away, for a couple of reasons. One, we didn't want copycats, and two, if a suspect happened to mention something that only the killer could know, we'd bag them fast. We'd established a tip line, and I was hopeful that someone, somewhere, was watching the news and would call in.

11

Saturday evening, 7 p.m.

AND SO THE EVENING DRAGGED ON. MY TEAM BEGAN
to drag too, but I knew they'd all rather get what they had
out of the way than have to come on Sunday. I sent
everyone off to get coffee and be back in ten minutes. I
also asked Corbin to bring me a cup, which he did. It was
awful. It must have been sitting there in the urn for
hours. Still, it was strong and better than nothing.

"Okay," I said when everyone had settled back down.
"Let's get this done and see if we can't be out of here at a
reasonable hour."

"Hear, hear," Jack muttered.

"How were the Michaels?" I asked Hawk, leaning my
elbows on the table and looking at him over the rim of
my cup.

"Not great," Hawk said. "They took it hard, obviously. The wife more so than the husband."

Anne snorted, and I gave her a sharp look. "He's leaving out the important part," she said flatly. "They didn't want us around."

Hawk grimaced at his partner and continued, "Anne's right. They were suspicious right off the bat. Once we told them why we were there, they calmed down a bit. They were both stunned and obviously grieving, but I could tell they still didn't trust us. Strange couple."

Anne nodded solemnly. "True. When we started asking questions about Jared's movements over the past several days, they claimed they knew nothing. When I mentioned his record and his misdemeanors, they clammed up completely. Greg Michaels was visibly upset."

To me, that wasn't really surprising. In fact, it was good to hear that the kid's foster parents cared enough about him to be defensive.

"Greg Michaels called Jared's brother, Chase," I said. "Did you know about that?"

Anne and Hawk shook their heads. Anne's eyes narrowed. "Chase has quite a rap sheet, right?"

"Right. I'm not sure that means much, though."

They both gave me a questioning look, so I continued, "I interviewed Chase Richards and, like the foster parents, he was protective of his little brother. He claimed he'd been keeping away from him, that he wanted him to have a chance to make something of himself."

"After they'd settled down and it hit them that they'd

lost him," Anne said, "Amy Michaels was a little more forthcoming. She confirmed that Jared had been in trouble, but she insisted that he was trying to do better."

I nodded and looked at Hawk, who seemed to be deep in thought.

"What's up, Hawk?" I asked.

"I'm a little surprised that Greg called the brother," he replied, glancing at his partner. "In fact, Greg insinuated that he thought Chase might be involved."

"Both Greg and Amy asked if we'd spoken to Chase," Anne said. "I assured them that we were going to—well, that you were going to. They seemed relieved about that —that a senior officer would be telling him—so I'm thinking the idea that Chase was involved was a real concern for them. You're sure he isn't a suspect?"

I nodded. "I don't think he could have killed his brother, but he did give me the name of that girl Herbert was supposed to have been with."

"You're talking about the girl Jasmine, right?" Anne asked.

"Yes, exactly."

I nodded, turned to Jack and said, "How did the canvassing go? Did you learn anything?"

"Not much, to be honest," he replied. "Like I mentioned earlier, it's a pretty rural neighborhood. Not many houses around, none within sight of the cemetery. And it's surrounded by trees."

"Anyone hear the shots?" Anne asked.

Jack shook his head. "No, which is not surprising, considering the remoteness of the area. Then again, a 30-

30 makes one hell of a bang. But no, though one neighbor said it wasn't uncommon to hear gunshots out that way. Several people in the neighborhood have their own shooting ranges on their property."

Anne looked at the whiteboard and said thoughtfully, "There's no way it could have been an accident, I suppose? A couple of drunks playing around with a rifle and pointing it in the wrong direction?"

"Nope. The shots were too accurate," I said. "There's no way someone accidentally shot Caroline Davis in the head and Jared Moore in the neck. Plus, it didn't explain why someone had up and dragged Jared's body around the truck and dumped it in the truck bed. No, this was deliberate."

I was so lost in my own thoughts that I almost missed Jack's next words. "...who lives next to the cemetery has had a few run-ins with your guy Herbert, the groundskeeper. Said he's eccentric but didn't peg him for a killer."

My eyes narrowed. "You didn't seem too hot on Herbert earlier on," I said.

"Yeah, well," he said. "There's something about the guy that just grinds my gears, Cap. He's entering a sacred space and telling people he can talk to their dead loved ones." He shook his head, his lips set.

Me? I totally understood. I felt much the same. The job of cemetery groundskeeper seemed *too* good a fit for someone like Brad Herbert, who took a particular interest in the dead. But did his weird interests make him a killer? We'd have to see.

In my heart, I knew it didn't. Dabbling in the occult was one thing. Murder was a whole other game, and it was one hell of a big leap from one to the other.

"This seems like a bust," Hawk finally said. From the way Anne was rubbing her silver-streaked temples, it was obvious she agreed.

"We could talk to their classmates," Jack said. "Talk to some of the kids who knew Caroline and Jared?"

I nodded slowly. "Yes, we could, but we can't do anything until Monday. I'm calling the superintendent Monday morning. I want to know who Jasmine is and just how deep into this witchcraft thing she is. If Caroline Davis was mixed up with Jasmine and whatever she was into, that might give us something to work with."

The atmosphere in the room had become... uncomfortable. No one, it seemed, wanted to jump on the occult bandwagon. Every team in the PD had to be careful of bringing up occult activity, or anything like it, because the press would spin it out of control. It would be the Salem witch trials all over again—accusations left and right.

"Where are we with ballistics?" I asked, knowing that Anne and Hawk had checked with the lab.

"Nowhere yet," Anne replied. "They're checking to see if they can determine the make and model of the weapon."

"Mike's still working it. He seemed frustrated when we spoke," Hawk added.

"No wonder," I said, "considering what he's had to deal with out there. The storm, and all."

I rubbed my eyes. "All right," I said. "I'm bushed. Let's get the hell out of here. Enjoy your Sunday off. You may not get another one for a while."

Slowly, they all rose to their feet and headed for the door, and then I was all alone with my thoughts. I sat there at the table, staring into the deep, dark remains of my coffee, too tired to get up. It had been an exhaustingly long and difficult day.

I looked at Samson. He gazed back at me with big, liquid brown eyes, and I melted.

"Okay, Sammy," I said. "Come on. It's time to go home."

And we did.

12

Sunday morning, 9 a.m.

I DIDN'T SLEEP WELL THAT NIGHT, TOSSING AND turning until well after two, then waking early at just after six. I was too tired to go for a run, so we settled for a short walk around the subdivision. *Sheesh,* I thought as we climbed the steps on our way back. *I'll be glad when we're moved.* "Then you'll be able to go in the backyard. Won't you, Sammy boy?"

He looked up at me and stood patiently while I unlocked the door, then pushed me out of the way and bunted the door open with his nose. Then he ran to the kitchen and downed half his bowl of water.

"Good boy, Sammy," I said. I always praised him when he drank and ate, hoping the praise would encourage him. No way did I want a finicky dog.

Anyway, it was just after nine when we returned that Sunday morning. I was determined to relax, take it easy and be up bright and early the following morning and ready to kill it—the case, I mean.

And I was determined to finish as much of my packing as I could, focusing on the last of my living room odds and ends, in the hopes that, in just a few days, we'd be moving into the new house.

And as I told you, I was more than ready for it. My apartment had served me well for as many years as I cared to remember, and I knew I was going to miss it. But it was also a stark, stale reminder of all of the tragedy I'd been witness to over the years, especially the death of Detective Lennie Miller, my one-time computer go-to guy who was murdered in the parking lot. So, it was time for a fresh start in at least one area of my life.

AROUND TEN THAT MORNING, I received a call from a Sergeant Dexter. He was heading up the small army of detectives that Chief Johnston had approved to comb through tips. He called to tell me they were already coming in. I, in turn, told him to sort and prioritize them and that I'd have someone from my team go through them on Monday morning.

Lunch was a quick and easy fried bologna sandwich —if you've never tried it, you should. They are delicious. And I poured myself a glass of red wine, also delicious. Sam had to make do with kibbles, and he didn't look too thrilled about it. Then, with sandwich and glass in hand, I went to the living room, plonked myself down on the couch, and Sammy jumped up beside me—not something

I usually condoned, but we both needed a break. He rested his head on my lap with a big sigh and looked up at me.

"Oh, I know," I murmured, clicking on the television. TV wasn't something I indulged in often because most of the content was mindless dross, but some nights, and even afternoons, mindless was what I needed.

Before I could find something to zone out on, even before I could take a bite of my sandwich or a sip of wine, my phone began buzzing.

"Damn!" I snapped.

I almost didn't answer it, but I did.

"Hello?"

"Kate! I have great news," my realtor, Benjamin, sang into the phone. *Geez, on a Sunday afternoon?* I thought, but then I smiled. He sounded enthusiastic.

"Hey, Ben," I said. "What's up?"

"The contractor took care of those two leaky skylights," he burbled, "so we can move the closing up to Tuesday if you want! I already have the paperwork written up."

I sat up, almost spilling wine on the couch. "Really? The sellers agreed to that?"

"Oh, they're the ones who offered, honey. They want to be off to Vermont ASAP."

"Okay, then. Yes. That would be perfect." I looked around at the boxes stacked everywhere, my heart beating a little bit faster at the thought of being in *my own* house.

Sammy pawed my leg.

Okay, *our* house.

"I'll email it over for a signature right now. Let's plan on Tuesday at noon?"

The thought of the case suddenly hit me like a ton of bricks. "I can do that, Ben, but it will be just for a quick walkthrough. I've got a lot going on."

"Oh, I know," he tWhittered. "It's been all over the news. No worries. I'll get there early and do my own run-through. If everything looks good, I'll leave you the key, and you can move in whenever you're ready!"

"Perfect, thanks again, Ben. I'll get everything signed and back to you as soon as the email comes through."

For a few moments after the call, all I could do was grin at Sammy.

"Tuesday, Sammyo. We'll be in our new home on Tuesday! Well, maybe... as long as nothing crazy comes up. How am I going to find the time to move into a new house and get settled with this case going on?"

Samson didn't answer. Instead, he laid his head back in my lap and looked up at me dolefully.

Shaking my head, I scrolled through the shows on Britbox until I found an old but well-liked British sitcom, knowing I'd probably be asleep on the couch minutes after I'd finished my sandwich and wine, but that's just what I wanted. I took a huge bite, ruffled Sammy's ears with my free hand and chewed contentedly.

Outwardly, I was at peace. Inwardly, my mind kept replaying the same sweeping imagery of the crime scene, the truck, the bodies, and the two overly curious boys in the tricked-out pickup truck. What should have been a peaceful but wild and beautiful place had been turned into a gut-wrenching, bloody crime scene.

Whatever had possessed Caroline and Jared to hang out in a cemetery that late at night, only God knew. *Was there really nowhere else they could go and be alone together?* I wondered.

When I was a kid, the list of hangouts was pretty long... but maybe Jared's reputation and Caroline's strict parents meant they *really* did have to keep things under wraps. What did their friends think about the two of them? Did they even know about their relationship?

Although Caroline hadn't kept it from her sister...

Then there was the whole possibility of witchcraft, or maybe something even more sinister, being involved. But from what I knew of witchcraft, it was generally a belief based on magic, not evil, unlike satanism. Like all things in life, though, there were a few people who ruined it for the many... that was where black magic came in.

My conversation with Chief Johnston came back to me.

"Don't you dare mention cults... or witchcraft, Kate. Or the occult. You know any mention of either would put us right in the deep end."

"I know, Chief, I know, I just... I just want you to be prepared for the possibility. I mean, even Mike was heading down that road."

"Kate, if anyone gets wind that you're thinking something that sinister might be involved..."

Everyone on the team was thinking it; that much was evident. But I had to agree with Johnston. It was too dangerous and way too soon to label it occult activity. Hell, we didn't even know if we were dealing with just one killer.

With a sigh, I turned to look at Samson, who was watching my plate intently.

"What do you think, Sam? Are we going to be able to solve this one?"

He lifted his head up off my lap, looked up at me and whined.

"Well," I said. "At least you and I are on the same page."

13

Monday morning, 8:30 a.m.

Jasmine

WE ARRIVED IN THE OFFICE EARLY THAT FOLLOWING Monday morning, but I wasn't the first in. Corbin, as usual, beat me to it and surprisingly, so did Anne Robar.

As soon as eight-thirty rolled around, I called the school's superintendent's office. The phone was answered by a Gloria Templeton, someone I didn't know, but as soon as I told her who I was and what I wanted, she put me through to Harris Stevens, the superintendent, whom I did know.

I told him what I needed and why. He quickly agreed and asked me to hold while he had Gloria check the files.

He was back a few moments later with the news that the past student's name was indeed Jasmine Hall. Then he asked if there was anything else I needed, and I told him I might need to interview some of the victim's classmates, to which he readily agreed so long as there was a counselor present, but I was to let him know in advance so he could give the school principal the heads-up.

"I appreciate that, Harris," I said. "Thank you, I will, and please tell Gloria I said thank you as well and that I'm sorry for bothering you both so early."

I hung up the phone and looked at Corbin, who'd been waiting patiently. He'd come in mid-way through the call. Anne was seated at the table, flipping through the files.

"Well," I said. "Now we know. Chase's Jasmine and Herbert's Jasmine Hall are one and the same. Chase and Jasmine were at school together. Jasmine stayed mostly out of trouble, except for a few times when she skipped out early. Not a bad kid, by all accounts. No red flags."

I looked up at the whiteboard. Anne had posted photos of Caroline, Jared and Chase. It looked pretty bare. Not what I was used to. But now we had a connection to add to the board; one I felt good about.

I filled Corbin in, and he looked relieved. "Doc couldn't help much," he said, ignoring Samson as the shepherd snuffled croissant crumbs from his pants. "Pretty much the same info he gave us at the scene. Caroline took a shot from a 30-30 rifle to the head, just above her ear, at which point we think Jared must have gotten out of the car and tried to run. He was shot in the neck, through and through, clipping the left carotid artery and the windpipe. He would have bled out fairly quickly."

So, I was right, I thought.

"Whoever did it," Corbin continued, "must have gone to the truck for some reason. Whatever it was, he picked Jared up and tossed him into the truck bed. Why he would do that is anybody's guess."

"Did Doc say if he was alive when he was moved?" I asked.

Corbin shrugged. "It's hard to tell, but Doc couldn't rule it out. Whoever did it, did it carefully. There weren't any marks or DNA evidence that he could find, except for a bruise forming on the back of Jared's head from being tossed in there."

Ugh.

"There's something else," Corbin said. "Remember we thought it was long-range?"

"Yeah—hard to imagine out there, through all those trees and the low light."

"Exactly. Doc touched base with ballistics, and they came to the conclusion that the shots were fired from closer than we thought. Caroline and Jared still didn't see their attacker; Caroline was looking forward when she was shot, and Jared was trying to run."

My shoulders sagged at the news. "Someone snuck up on them?"

"Or was already there, waiting."

I frowned. "But that would mean they had to know Caroline and Jared were going to be there."

Corbin nodded and scratched his chin, and I could tell that he hadn't quite worked that part out either. "Either that or they were followed," he muttered.

"Doc put time of death between midnight and one-thirty in the morning," he said.

I thought back to my conversation with Sarah Davis and her parents. "That's a few hours after Caroline snuck out. So either they were at that cemetery the whole time, or out and about elsewhere."

Where would two teens go on a Friday night? I wondered.

It was around nine o'clock when Captain Russo De León, head of the K-9 unit, knocked on my door and entered. He was carrying a K-9 dog harness and a badge in a plastic cover.

"You and the pup got a minute, Captain?" he asked.

"Sure," I said, getting up from my desk. "What's up?"

"The chief told me late Friday that, if you're going to keep Samson with you all the time, he needs to be sworn in. It will make it easier for you when you're doing your interviews."

"Well... that's nice of him," I said, surprised, "but do you really do that, swear them in?"

He grinned and looked at Sam, who cocked his head and stared up at him. "Only the smart ones," he said. "It's just a bit of fun. You want to try?"

"Sure, but let's get the rest of my team in first. They won't want to miss it. Anne, would you go get them, please?"

She did, and five minutes later, we were ready to begin and set my phone to video to record the ceremony.

De León had Samson sit in front of him and said, "Samson, raise your right paw."

Samson looked up at him but didn't move.

"Sam," I said. "Paw!"

He raised his left paw as he did when we high-fived.

"Good enough," De León said, then continued, "Samson, do you solemnly swear that you will carry out your duties as a sworn police officer to the best of your ability?"

Samson looked first at me, then back at De León and damned if he didn't bark and then lowered his paw. I was stunned.

"He's done that before," Hawk said in my ear, clapping. Everybody clapped and cheered as De León hooked the badge to Sam's collar. But then, I had a sudden chilling thought.

"He still belongs to me, right?" I asked.

"Yes, of course. As I said, it's honorary and just for your own convenience. His badge number is H274. The H is for honorary. He's a smart one. Enjoy, Captain. Oh, and by the way, that's the biggest harness we had. I hope it fits."

THE SITUATION ROOM was bustling with a small team of uniformed officers manning the tipline. Samson happily trotted into the fray, wagging his tail low and butting up against anyone who even looked his way.

"The tips are pouring in," Dani said excitedly. She and Cooper had arrived at eight, although when working cases like this, we never knew when we'd be leaving the office.

I smiled tightly. "That's great."

A small part of me, the "new detective" part, was hopeful. But my years of experience taught me that tiplines usually filled the days with rumors and false leads. Still, every tip we received, no matter how outlandish it might seem, had to be worked. Scrutinizing the group, I could see they were struggling to keep up, so I decided I'd talk to Chief Johnston later about adding some more bodies. I didn't want my team wasting their time on wild goose chases; better to have others do the sorting.

"Hey, Cap. Check this out." Cooper gestured to me. I stepped over to the desk where he was watching Officer Mendez on a call. Mendez's notes were, thankfully, legible.

B. Herbert, at cemetery after hours multiple times, usually walking not working—

"Interesting," I said.

Cooper grinned. "There are a lot of tips coming in about Brad Herbert."

I looked at Corbin. "How?" I asked Cooper. "Where are they coming from? There can't be more than a couple of dozen people living in that area."

"Oh, they're from all over," Cooper replied. "Seems like everyone agrees that Herbert is a weird bird. He hasn't won himself any glowing reviews, that's for sure."

"That's all well and good," Corbin said. "But are any of the tips about him actually helpful?"

Cooper shrugged. Dani shook her head. "Aside from confirming that he's a weirdo, no."

"Hmm," I said. "The tipster—that last one—said that Herbert was often at the cemetery after hours—"

"Cap!"

My thought was interrupted by Corbin, who nodded in the direction of the elevators, where an officer was standing, looking at me with his hand up. With him was a pretty young woman. And when I say pretty, I mean almost enviously so. She had the looks of those girls you see in shampoo ads. Her hair was... beautiful: long, thick, lustrous, shining. She had a heart-shaped face, a pixyish, upturned nose and almond-shaped, dark eyes. After I gave the officer a nod, she walked confidently across the situation room toward us; all eyes were on her.

"I'm looking for Captain Gazzara," she said, glancing between myself and Dani before figuring out that it must be me. Probably because I was beginning to look my age, and half-dead.

"That would be me," I said with a nod. "How can I help you?"

The young woman held out a slim hand, palm down, with strange symbols tattooed on her knuckles.

"I'm Jasmine Hall," she said as I took her hand and shook it. "I saw the tipline on the news, and I was going to call. Then I thought better of it and decided to come and talk to you instead. Is that all right?"

It was more than all right. It saved us the trouble of going to see her.

"Of course," I replied. "Come with me, Ms. Hall. Corbin?"

I took her to an interview room and asked her to sit down. Then I introduced Corbin and told her I was going to record the interview for the record. She had no problem with that. In fact, she looked pleased with the idea.

I sat across from her with the table between us. Corbin sat next to me, his eyes locked on Jasmine, narrowed, as if he was trying to see through her beauty. And she was undeniably beautiful. But then she spoke, and the effect was ruined.

"The goddess told me to come speak with you," she said.

I... actually puffed my cheeks and blew air out between my lips, and then I realized what I'd done and smiled at her.

Samson, wearing his new K-9 officer harness, had followed me into the room and was circling around behind me, sniffing around. He barely glanced at Jasmine, which was a good sign, I supposed. Corbin somehow managed to keep his composure and didn't even blink at her bizarre declaration.

"I'm sorry, uh... Can you repeat that, please?" I asked, more for something to say than to hear it again. And I was wondering what other weird stuff would come out of that pretty mouth.

"Like I said, I saw the tipline and the goddess told me I should speak to you, but I like to do these things in person. So, here I am," she said brightly.

"Because?" I asked, again stumped for words.

"I wanted to get a look at you," she continued, then looked at Corbin. "And you too, Sergeant Russell."

Corbin simply smiled at her and said nothing.

"So, you have something you want to tell us," I said. "What would that be?"

Jasmine turned from Corbin and looked at me, and, oh, did I mention her eyes were violet? But that wasn't her real eye color, of course. I'd seen colored contacts before, worn by models, but until then, I didn't know anyone who actually wore them. On Jasmine they were striking, especially as she was clothed from head to toe in black.

Even if I hadn't spoken to Chase Richards and heard his theories about witchcraft, I probably would've pegged the girl as a witch, or at least a wannabe.

"Yes," she said simply. "First, I should tell you that I know you spoke to Brad Herbert yesterday, and I wanted to confirm that he was with me Friday night at my house."

"All—right," I said. "And what were you two doing, exactly?"

"I was performing a ritual," she explained. She said it as if it was the most natural thing to be doing, like baking cookies or watching a ball game.

"I'm sorry, Jasmine," I said. "I'm not familiar with your..." I closed my eyes, opened them again, and continued, "...interests. Would you please explain, in detail, exactly what you and Mr. Herbert were doing?"

She looked amused but nodded and said, "I have a

gorgeous brook on my property, and water is a wonderful conductor. Some of Brad's crystals have been picking up negative energy these last few weeks, and I needed to neutralize them."

"What kind of crystals?" I asked.

"Smoky quartz," she replied.

"Smoky quartz?" I said. "I'm not understanding. Can you explain?"

"Yes, of course," she replied. "So smoky quartz crystals have the power to help you deal with fear and negative energy. They are good for the soul and for emotional well-being. They can even lift the cloak of depression. I carry one with me all the time. See?"

She reached into a pocket and produced a beautiful, polished, flat round stone, and handed it to me.

"That's a thumb, or worry, stone," she said. "I wouldn't go anywhere without it. You put them in running water to 'cleanse' them, and doing so by moonlight also 'charges' them. But the charge only lasts so long. What Brad and I were doing was... just general upkeep. We cleanse our crystals often. Most people do."

"So you were putting them in the water?" I asked, handing it back to her.

"Yes, exactly," she said in reply to my question, then, "No, please. Keep it. I have another. I hope it serves you well," she said, smiling.

I hesitated, then said, "I'm sorry. I can't accept it. It would be against policy."

She nodded and replied, "I understand, but you should get one... I think you might need it, seriously."

Now that did make my skin crawl. I handed the crystal back to her.

"Why were you doing it at night, after midnight?" Corbin asked.

"Oh. Yes. Well, for two reasons," she said. "You see, I work at Sullivan's Pub and my shift didn't end until eleven. I usually get home just before midnight. Brad arrived just after me, at about... oh, twelve-fifteen or so. The other reason is, as I told you, the cleansing is best done by moonlight."

And there it was. It added up, aside from the crystal cleansing thing. But, to each his own, as they say. And, if what she said was true, I could eliminate Brad Herbert from my slim list of suspects.

Jasmine, I knew, was only nineteen, so she wasn't a bartender.

"You're a waitress?" I asked.

She nodded. "Yes. I work mostly morning shifts. But one of the other waitresses called in sick on Friday, so I picked up her shift instead."

Out of the corner of my eye, I could see Corbin making a note to check that detail with the manager of Sullivan's.

"Jasmine," I said, "is there anyone who can corroborate that you were home that night and that you had company?"

She laughed. "You can ask my neighbor, Laura Maxwell. She's always complaining even though there's a privacy fence up. Oh, and my parents, of course."

"You live with your parents?" I asked, wondering

how the hell they felt about the creepy cemetery groundskeeper hanging around their home and daughter after midnight.

She happily gave us her address. All the time twisting an amethyst ring around her finger; one of many. Samson, by then, had settled down at the edge of the table and was watching her.

"What a beautiful dog," the girl commented, smiling at Samson but not moving to pet him. He twitched an ear as if he knew we were talking about him.

"Thank you," I replied.

"Is he yours, or is he a police dog?"

"He's mine," I said. "Why do you ask?"

"Because you two have a soul connection, you know."

She said it warmly, and I couldn't help but glance at Corbin, then at Samson. As much as I hated to admit it, I knew she was right. I felt it was fate that Sammy and I had found each other.

"Jasmine, do you and Brad ever do... rituals at the cemetery?"

"Oh, no. No, we both respect that space," she replied. "The dead must be allowed to rest in peace."

Corbin frowned. "Oh? We've been told, by people who know him, that Mr. Herbert talks to them, the people in the cemetery. He told them he did."

For the first time, she looked a little uncomfortable. She shifted in her chair and said, "Well, yes. He does, but Brad can't really help that, can he? They come to him when they come, you know?"

All right, I thought. *Let's play along.*

"Do they mind that he talks about them?" I asked.

Again, she looked uncomfortable, a slight grimace on her face. "I don't have Brad's abilities, so I really can't say. I don't think those who have passed would be upset, but... Well, I think it's just... Well, *I* wouldn't bother the living with it, you know?"

"I think I understand, but can you explain what you mean, please?"

She huffed and began spinning a different ring, this one with a stone that looked milky and smooth. "Brad has one foot in the world of the living and one in the world of the dead, so he doesn't always notice when people are upset. Some people just aren't ready to hear the messages their loved ones want to pass on."

I nodded, though it was hard to wrap my head around what she was trying to explain. And then I remembered what Chase had said about Jared being concerned that Caroline was involved with Jasmine somehow.

"Jasmine," I said, locking eyes with her, "did you know Caroline Davis?"

Sadness flashed across her features quickly. "Yes, of course, and I thought... I mean, I was hoping it wasn't her, but I thought it might be. She liked that cemetery."

"Did she go there often? Just with her boyfriend, or..."

Jasmine looked surprised at the mention of Jared.

"I thought Caroline was trying to keep her relationship with Jared secret. Nobody was supposed to know about them."

"Caroline's family told us about their relationship. And..." I wasn't sure I should be giving away so much information. The media had, to that point, kept the teens' names out of the story since they were minors, and out of respect for the families, but I took a leap of faith and said, "...I'm sorry to tell you that Jared was the other victim."

She raised a hand to her open mouth in shock, her eyes wide. "Oh, no. Oh, poor Caroline." Her grief seemed genuine, and I had to ask.

"Just how well did you and Caroline know each other?"

Jasmine sniffed, blinking repeatedly to stop from tearing up. "We were friends. Good friends, but only just recently. We met just after I graduated."

"How did you meet?" I asked.

"She came into Sullivan's sometimes with her family. One day, she told me she liked my necklace." She reached under her neckline and pulled out a delicate chain with a pendant. Something cast in resin...

Corbin and I leaned forward to get a better look.

The pendant was made up of tiny blue flowers with what looked like an animal bone amid them. I frowned and looked at her, my eyebrows raised in question.

Jasmine smiled. "It's a mouse's femur," she explained happily, as if that wasn't the strangest thing I'd heard of, ever. "Caroline and I got chatting, and we found we had similar... interests."

"The rituals?" Corbin asked.

Jasmine pursed her lips as if she didn't want to tell us

about it, which seemed odd because she'd been so forthcoming.

"Caroline was an intuitive person," she said evasively. "She understood that everything, we humans included, is inextricably linked to nature, that whatever we put out comes back threefold—"

I could sense a rant coming, so I interrupted her, "Did Caroline ever participate in any of these rituals with you?"

She shook her head. "No, we didn't know each other that well yet. But I could see that the goddess was calling her, pulling her... Like I said, the cemetery was one of her favorite spots."

Was it just me, or was it weird that everyone involved in this case so far seemed to love that cemetery?

"Oh, and that reminds me," she said, perking up again, her violet eyes locked onto mine. "The message. I'm supposed to tell you that more death is coming."

"I... I'm sorry?" I said, stunned. That was absolutely the last thing I'd been expecting.

"More death is coming," she said emphatically, her eyes sad now that she'd seen my reaction.

Corbin was sitting bolt upright, his back straight as an arrow. And I wondered if what we were hearing was making his skin crawl, too.

"Who gave you that message?" I asked, maybe a little too harshly.

Jasmine shrugged, spinning the ring on her finger faster. "No one. It just came to me when I saw the story on the news last night. I came down to tell you because you should know, and be prepared."

The room was silent for a few beats as Corbin and I gathered ourselves. Jasmine seemed put out, either uncomfortable with how we'd reacted or that she'd "passed on" the message at all.

Did I believe her? Hell no. Well, maybe, somewhere deep in my gut, something was telling me to beware.

"And that's it?" I asked. "That's all you can tell us? You don't know where the message came from or from whom?"

"Yes, that's all I can tell you," she replied, shaking her head.

I looked at Corbin. He nodded. It was time to wrap up the interview.

"Jasmine," I said. "Can you think of anyone, anyone at all, that might have a grudge against Caroline or Jared? Anyone that might have wanted to hurt either of them?"

Again, she slowly shook her head, her eyes locked on mine, and said, "No. No one I can think of."

"Well," I said, rising to my feet. "That should do it, for now. Thank you, Jasmine. We appreciate you coming in. You've been a great help. We may want to reach out to you again, if that's all right."

She nodded eagerly, though her eyes seemed filled with sadness.

Corbin asked her for her phone number, thanked her, and told her he'd see her out.

"Come on, Samson," I said quietly, burying my fingers comfortingly in the fur at the scruff of his neck.

More death is coming, she'd said. I hoped with all my heart she was wrong.

"Captain Gazzara. Kate," she said at the door. "It is Kate, isn't it? You never did ask me *how* I know things."

I narrowed my eyes and frowned at her, wondering what the hell her game was.

"All right," I replied. "I'll bite. How did you know about the message?"

"I'm a witch," she said. "Don't forget to get yourself a crystal." And with that, she quickly turned and walked out into the hallway.

14

Monday morning, 10:30 a.m.

SAMMY AND I RETURNED TO MY OFFICE WHILE
Corbin escorted Jasmine Hall to the front entrance.

I was... Hell, I don't know what it was. It had been
my first encounter with a so-called witch, and I didn't
quite know what to make of it, or her.

On the one hand, I was impressed by her confidence,
her worldliness, her... otherworldliness, and her stun-
ningly attractive presence and personality. I'd never met
anyone like her, and I had a lingering want to know her
better. Did I believe her? Yes. I believed that she and
Herbert were indeed together doing whatever in the
moonlight. Oh, my God. What am I saying—that I
believe they were casting spells? Did I believe her
message? I want to say no, emphatically no, but I have to
tell you, deep down inside, I wondered.

Half-hour later, with my jaw aching from grinding my teeth, I sat back in my chair, stretched my arms over my head, tilted my head back as far as it would go, stretched out my legs, closed my eyes and tried to relax, to ease the muscles... but, nope. One more glance at Mike Willis' report sitting in the folder on my desk and I bore down on my poor molars again.

Inside the folder there was... nothing.

Well, not exactly nothing. More like a detailed ten pages explaining that Mike Willis and his small team had found *virtually* nothing.

No unidentified fingerprints anywhere on the vehicle or the kids. Even though Jared had been dragged to the truck bed, there were no prints on him, either. Which meant whoever did it must have been wearing gloves. Nor had Mike or Doc found any foreign fibers on either of the bodies.

The chipped glass didn't tell us anything helpful, either. Just the obvious—that someone had shot Caroline through the open passenger side window. That detail made me think that it hadn't been an opportunistic shooting. The chip in the glass, the wound in Caroline's head and the spot where the bullet had been found all indicated a line of fire. Mike and his team had followed it for several hundred yards into the woodland but had found nothing. It was one hell of a shot, especially in the semi-darkness. The shot that killed Jared was even better, considering the boy was on the move. So, I thought, *we're looking for a hunter. Someone who's a great shot. Someone proficient in woodcraft. Hmm... Ex-military? A sniper? A park ranger? A hunter?*

"And it had to have been planned, right, Sammy?"

He looked up at me and tilted his head.

"Think about it," I said. "There's no way an opportunistic killer just 'happened' to be in *that* right place at the right time, *after midnight.*"

When I saw the report on the kids' cell phones, I became a little more optimistic. Cell phones, especially those belonging to teens, could be a hothouse full of clues: all kinds of dirt, rumors, nasty snarky texts. Most kids these days don't delete anything. They leave it all festering there on that wicked little device.

But a quick scan of the page had me grinding my teeth again. The tech team hadn't found anything of interest on the phones at all. Just the typical messages. They'd discovered that Jared's number was saved in Caroline's contacts as "Carrie," probably to fool her parents if they checked her phone.

Willis ended his report with several paragraphs that provided details of the scene and how the rain had destroyed most of it: flattened the grass, washed most of it out, including what looked like a tire track, and so on. He also noted that they'd found a strip of six condoms in the truck's glove compartment, indicating that Caroline and Jared were probably on intimate terms.

"Hey, Cap."

I looked up to see Corbin standing in the doorway.

Samson immediately got to his feet and went to him, wagging his tail slowly.

"Hey," I replied. "Come on in and take a seat." I must have sounded depressed.

"That bad?" he asked as he sat down at the table.

I tossed the file to him, and for the next several minutes, while I checked my emails, Corbin scanned through the pages, frowning and shaking his head.

Finally, he closed the file, looked across the desk at me and said, "Not much, huh?"

I snorted. "Not much? There's *nothing*. Nothing useful at all, nothing that points to someone we've already spoken to or anyone new." It was hard not to rant in situations like this.

"What about the tire tracks?" He flipped open the file again and flipped through the pages. "Willis says here that they found tire tracks that weren't completely destroyed by the rain. 'Made by a dual rear-wheel vehicle.'"

"Well, there's that, I suppose," I said, "but they were full of water. There was no way he could get a print."

"It could be significant, though," he said. "That cemetery doesn't get a lot of use."

"A lot of use?" I said, making a face. "You make it sound as if the inhabitants are getting out of bed and going on a walkabout. But I know what you mean, and you're right," I said. "Jeff Harper was quick to tell us he rarely saw anybody else at the cemetery. It's an older site, rarely used anymore. His wife's there only because her family's buried there and she wanted to continue the tradition. That's what he said, anyway."

But Corbin was right; the headstones were all worn with age. Not smooth, but pock-marked, many of the names and dates impossible to read. And it had been overgrown in a wild, even beautiful sort of way. Brad Herbert was caring for it, yes, but not really sticking to the true definition of the word "maintaining."

"Yep," I said thoughtfully. "There's not much traffic through the place, that's for sure... Though maybe, judging from the condoms in Jared's truck, it was used by the kids as a spot for lovers. It's certainly private enough."

Corbin nodded, staring at the file with a bemused look on his face, then shook his head and looked up at me questioningly.

"What are we doing here, Corbin? We have almost nothing to go on. No real suspects. Just a couple of weirdos, a couple of curious kids with attitudes, and not a single lead. Jeff Harper's not even a consideration. Chase Richards isn't exactly a gleaming example of citizenship, but I get the impression he cared about his brother. And Greg and Amy Michaels don't trust the cops."

"I don't know," Corbin said. "But something has to give, and soon. The press are going to be all over it before we know it."

"Can we be missing something?" I asked. "We must be, unless..."

"Unless what?" Corbin asked.

"Unless it's a random shooter," I said. "I sure as hell hope not because if it is, we're screwed. If it's random, then it was just a crime of opportunity, a killer who happened upon two teenage kids out having a little fun. Well, as I said, then we're screwed."

"It's possible, I suppose," Corbin said, obviously not liking the idea. "How do you want to handle it, Kate? We have to do something."

I nodded, then got up and started pacing, trying to think, hoping my thoughts would work themselves out.

"What about those two kids in the truck we met out there?" I asked. "D'you think they might have had something to do with it?"

Corbin made a face. He was obviously skeptical of the idea.

"I doubt it," he said. "I don't think they have enough brains to be stupid."

I sucked air in through my teeth, making a hissing noise. Samson looked up at me, startled.

"You may be right," I said. "Let's get Hawk and Robar back out there; canvass the area again. This time I want them to check for rifles. Particularly 30-30 rifles. If they find any, we need to bring them in for ballistic comparison. So let's start there."

Corbin nodded as he wrote in his notebook.

"Okay," I said, squinting out the window. "that's something, for now at least. In the meantime, you and I will head back out to the cemetery. It should have dried out a bit by now and I want to get another look at the place, try and get a feel for it while it's dry."

Corbin stood, already preoccupied.

"Sounds good," he said. "I'll meet you out back. I'm

going to hand this off to Hawk. What d'you want Cooper, Dani and Jack to do?"

I thought for a few seconds before answering. "There's no point in sending everyone out there," I said. "There's only a couple of dozen residences, at the most. Have them help out on that drive-by that came in last night, for now. I'll see you down at my car."

15

Monday morning, 11:15 a.m.

IT WAS A LITTLE AFTER ELEVEN-FIFTEEN WHEN WE drove through the cemetery gates. It was, as I expected, deserted. A cold wind was blowing and the long grass, now revived by the downpour two days earlier, was standing tall and waving in the stiff breeze, as were the tops of the trees that surrounded the cemetery.

The drive to the crime scene was rougher than I remembered it, probably because I'd walked it the first time. Jared's truck had, of course, been removed, but the yellow crime scene tapes were still in place, fluttering in the wind.

We exited the car and I buttoned up my jacket before letting Samson out. When I did, he immediately bounded away toward the trees.

It was quiet there, desolate, and I shivered as I gazed around at the trees and ancient headstones.

"It's peaceful here, don't you think?" Corbin said.

"It's frickin' creepy, is what I think," I replied.

But he was right. Now that the two dozen or so offi-cers and crime scene techs were gone, the cemetery did have a certain appeal. And I found it hard to imagine that people would rather be buried in the city, in the busy, cramped acreages situated among the traffic and exhaust. This was better. Quieter. More... natural feeling, and I, though I'd yet to meet him, could understand Brad Herbert's affinity with his dead community. Even so, I had to wonder about the guy. Was he nuts? Or was he just over-imaginative?

We stood for a moment gazing at the crime scene: me with my hands in my jacket pockets, Corbin with his hands in his pants pockets. We must have looked like a couple of idiots.

"All right, Sergeant," I said, "let's do this."

Corbin nodded, then pointed. "We know Jared's truck was there. Harper was parked over there." He gestured toward where Lauren Harper's headstone was, and a couple of lines from her epitaph came into my mind:

You will remember
when this is blown over...

Sheesh, I thought. *I can't imagine it blowing over anytime soon.*

By then, Samson was nowhere in sight, and I began to worry that I might have lost him. But I put that out of my mind for the moment and concentrated on the scene.

"Okay," I said, "so the bed of the truck was here, and

hood here." I looked up and looked to the west. "That means the shots came from somewhere over there." I pointed. "And the state park boundary is a few hundred yards over that way, too."

Corbin and I looked off into the trees.

"The tree line's closer than we thought, right?" he asked, taking a few steps in that direction. "We thought initially it was long-range."

"Well, it is long-range, but yeah. Mike Willis and ballistics agree; it's closer than we thought."

Corbin half-turned back toward me. "So did anyone go into the trees?"

I nodded. "Yes. Willis and his team searched the woods to try and find out where the shots came from, but they had no luck. And, knowing Mike as I do, I don't think he would have missed anything."

"You got that right," Corbin said, eyeing the tall grass. It was almost knee-high. "Might be worth taking a look, though."

I nodded and said, "If you think it's worthwhile." Then I took a few steps toward the trees, wondering where Samson was.

"You okay?" Corbin called back.

"Yes, I'm fine. Keep going."

I called, "Sammy. Where are you? Come here, boy!"

He came loping toward me, leaping over the tall grass in huge bounds, his tongue hanging out the side of his mouth.

I trudged ahead, Samson running this way and that, his nose to the ground, trying to catch up with Corbin.

He was shorter than me by several inches but somehow seemed able to move faster and easier through the grass.

Eventually, he stopped and turned, squinting back toward where Jared's truck would have been, took several steps to his right, then two more, stopped, looked behind him, then at where the truck had been. Then he put his hands on his hips and waited for me to join him.

"I think the shots would've come from somewhere around here," he said. "Doc was thinking it was further back, but my guess, from how the bullet entered and left, would be around here."

"All right," I said, and we started walking slowly in an ever-widening circle, our eyes on the ground. Years of leaf litter had built up and been packed down, but it was all the same dull brown color, so one could hope any anomalies would stand out.

"All right," I said again after several minutes, pausing to look deep into the forest. "Booker T. Washington State Park is that way. How did they get in here? Not through these trees, I shouldn't think," I murmured to myself.

Corbin overheard me and said, "Could've walked in."

I pursed my lips and looked in that direction. "From the road? Not hardly. There are those tire marks, though, so he could have driven in and walked out here, I suppose, but I'm thinking the kids would have seen him, right? Pity Mike couldn't get tire prints."

I looked back toward the crime scene and said, "The perp must have come in from the woods. Either that or he was already here, waiting for them. But that would mean he knew they were coming and, as far as I know, the only person who knew Caroline was meeting with Jared that night was her sister. So, he couldn't have known, and that brings us back to the random killer idea, and I'm not buying that."

Corbin looked at me and raised his eyebrows. "Well, in that case, the only answer is that someone must have known they'd be here. If not, we have some crazy clown wandering around this forest, with a rifle, in the dead of night, and you're right; that makes absolutely no sense."

"So who?" I said. "Who could have known?"

"Beats me," he replied.

It was at that moment I heard a low rumbling sound and I looked up, frowning. At first, I thought it was a car engine, but then I saw Samson, some twenty or so yards away, back near the crime scene, the hackles along his back were standing up, and he was growling.

Corbin and I exchanged a glance, and I high-kneed it back toward him, where he was pacing back and forth, his nose to the ground, growling.

As I approached, I looked down at the ground and noticed that the dirt was scuffed and the grass broken. Two more steps and I saw what was bothering Samson. A single tire track, smooth, still with water in the bottom. Even so, I could tell that whoever had been driving the vehicle had spun the rear tires; the muddy track was smooth with little detail.

"Hey, Corbin. Over here," I called.

"Good boy," he said when he reached us, ruffling Samson's ears.

"These must be the tracks Willis wrote up in the report," I said.

Corbin nodded slowly. "Yep. Dual rear wheels. Whoever made these tracks must have been in one hell of a hurry... But there's a problem."

"Yes," I said. "If a truck that big was standing here, those two kids would have seen it, and they wouldn't have come anywhere near it, not unless..."

"They knew who it was," we both said together.

We looked at one another, me smiling. It wasn't much, but it *was* something. We were looking for someone with a truck with dual rear wheels. That was good, but not so good too. Every manufacturer I could think of made models with dual rear wheels.

"Those two rednecks," I said. "What were they driving? D'you remember?"

"It was a Ford 250, red, with single rear wheels."

"Damn!" I said.

Before either of us could say more, my cell rang, startling me. I looked at the screen and said, "This is the call we've been waiting for."

"Hello?"

"Hey, Kate, it's Peggy. Sorry to have taken so long getting back to you. It's a circus around here."

"No problem, Peg. Thanks for getting back to me. I'm sure you're busy. I'm going to put you on speaker so my partner, Sergeant Corbin Russell, can hear."

"Busy? You can say that again," she said. "Hey, I guess you're reaching out about the case that was on the news the other night, right? The two teens just outside Booker T?"

"Yes. I am, and I know it's out of your jurisdiction, but you deal with more of these remote cases than I do. Any idea what or who we should be looking for here?"

She was silent for a few moments, but it was a weighty silence. She was making a decision.

"If it were me, I'd check out Nate Rogan. He's an ex-con. He lives close to your crime scene, and he's on our radar."

I frowned. "What makes you think he might be good for it?"

"Well," Peggy said. "He only got out of jail about a month ago. He went down for assault with a deadly weapon. Inside the park. He got fifteen but got out early."

"How come he was released early?" I asked.

"As I said, he was in for fifteen years, but he cut himself a deal that got him out on parole. To be honest, I'm not sure what exactly got him released, Kate. But from what I remember of Rogan, he's no joke, so be careful."

"Do you know where he lives?" I asked.

"I do," she replied and gave me the address.

I thanked her for the info, hung up, and looked at Corbin, my lips pursed.

"That sounds promising," he said lightly.

"It does," I replied. "Come on, Sammy."

But something was nagging me. "If he lives only a mile away from here, wouldn't Jack have run into him while he was canvassing the area?"

"You would have thought so," Corbin replied. "But I don't remember seeing the name on his list, but it's worth a second visit. You want to give it a try? I can pull up his sheet in the cruiser."

"Let's do it," I said, loading Sam into the car and fitting him up with his badge and harness.

16

NATHANIEL ROGAN'S PROPERTY WAS DISTURBINGLY close to the cemetery.

Rogan's driveway was a long, narrow dirt track. There was a sign nailed to the trunk of a tree that read, "Private Property. Stay Out!"

"Let's drive on up there," I said uneasily. "I want to have the car close at hand, just in case."

The cruiser bumped and jerked up the driveway. The trees gave way to a surprisingly tidy but small lawn and a really nice-looking cabin. In fact, it almost looked like something out of a realty magazine. *How does an ex-con afford digs like this?* I wondered.

Samson, in the cramped back seat, panted and moved around restlessly, his breath fogging up the windows.

To the right of the cruiser, between us and the cabin, a rugged-looking blond guy in a stained t-shirt was chopping firewood. He'd obviously heard us coming because he was standing there, gripping the handle of an ax in both hands.

My goodness, the man was tall and powerfully built. At almost six feet, I towered over many of my coworkers, but even at a distance, I could tell that Rogan had a good five or six inches on me.

"Ready?" Corbin asked quietly, checking his holster. It was always unnerving to face an ex-con. Even more so in such a remote area with the said con holding an ax. And while Peggy hadn't given us much info on Rogan, his rap sheet told quite the tale.

According to his file, Rogan had done fifteen years in prison for assault with a deadly weapon when he was just nineteen; the deadly weapon being a hunting knife.

But that wasn't all; he hadn't exactly been a model prisoner. He'd been a fighter, a leader, while he was inside. Which was why I was surprised he'd been granted parole.

So, knowing what he was didn't make me feel any better about being on his property. A hard ass like Rogan is likely to shoot first and ask questions after.

The sound of the car doors shutting echoed in the small clearing. Yes, I figured he could have heard the shots from the cemetery.

Rogan stood there, slowly shaking his head. He released his left hand from the ax handle and let the tool dangle at his side. And, by the look on his face, it was clear he wasn't happy to see us.

"Oh no," he said as we stepped out of the car with our IDs in our hands.

His voice was low and gruff and didn't quite match up to his scrappy, lean appearance. A smattering of blond chest hair peeked out over the round neck of his t-shirt.

"No, no, no. I already talked to the other cop who came out here. I'm not talking no more."

"Mr. Rogan," Corbin said calmly, holding up his badge. "We just want a minute of your time. Just a few questions and we'll be on our way, okay?"

Rogan heaved a huge sigh, obviously unhappy with the idea, but he nodded, took the ax in both hands, swung it, buried the blade deep in his chopping block, and came over to us.

"I told the other cop," he said angrily. "I don't know nothin' about what happened over there. Nothin', and I don't have no answers to your questions. I'm not doing anythin' wrong—"

"No one says you are, Mr. Rogan," I said. "I'm Captain Gazzara, Chattanooga PD. This is Sergeant Russell. We just have a few questions."

Rogan ground his teeth, eyes flitting back and forth between Corbin and me.

"I been goin' to all my meetings," Rogan said quietly. "You can ask my PO, Hector Robles."

"You're aware of what happened at the cemetery?" I asked, biding time.

"Yes. And I had nothing to do with them two kids," he snapped.

"Where were you between midnight and one-thirty on Saturday morning, Mr. Rogan?" I asked.

Rogan nodded and rolled his shoulders. "I was here."

"Alone?" I asked. I could tell by the look on his face that I was rubbing him the wrong way.

"I was alone."

Great. I knew where this was going.

"So no one can corroborate that?" I said.

He shrugged. "My dogs, maybe, if they could talk. But no. I keep to myself. My nearest neighbor is almost a mile away."

"Do you own a firearm, Mr. Rogan? A rifle?"

I already knew the answer to that. As a convicted felon, he wasn't allowed to own a firearm of any kind. But I watched his face, trying to gauge his reaction.

"Now you know the answer to that, Captain. No, I don't, but I used to. A Winchester. Back before I went away."

"What happened to it?" Corbin asked.

"It's at my parents' house. I sold it to my dad."

"And where do they live?"

He shot me another glance, obviously uncomfortable. "Across town. Out near Ridgeside."

"The address?" I said.

He gave it to me, and Corbin made a note of it.

Just then, frenzied barking broke out and we all turned to look at the cruiser. A black and tan coonhound, accompanied by an athletic-looking beagle, were circling the cruiser, snapping at the windows.

"Hey!" Corbin called out, not happy to see the coon-hound with his front paws scrabbling at the door.

Samson, in the back seat, ignored the two dogs. But I saw him looking at the hound as if to say, *This one is crazy,* and I smiled.

Rogan whistled, a sharp and high sound, and the dogs backed off. The beagle trotted off back toward the woods, looking over its shoulder at us as he went. The coon-hound moved reluctantly away from the car, circled it one more time, then he, too, disappeared into the trees.

"If there's nothing else, I think you should leave," Rogan said. The words sounded more like a warning than a suggestion, so I decided not to push our luck any further. That Rogan was a dangerous man was undeniable.

"One more thing, Mr. Rogan," I said. "Did you hear anything that night?"

"What d'you mean? I told you. I was asleep."

"Oh, come on," Corbin said. "This place is less than a thousand yards from that cemetery. Three shots from a 30-30 in the middle of the night. They would have awakened the dead."

No pun intended, I thought.

"I din't hear nothin'," he snapped.

"All right," I said. "Thank you again for your time, Mr. Rogan." I smiled pleasantly. I'd be reaching out to his PO, and he knew it.

He didn't answer, not even to say goodbye as we turned back to the cruiser.

"What d'you think?" I asked as Corbin turned the car around and we drove away.

Corbin shook his head, frowning. "I don't know, Kate. I don't think it was him."

"Why not?"

Corbin took a moment to gather his thoughts and then said, "Don't get me wrong. I think the guy's capable of just about anything. But I just don't think he fits the mold. All those years ago, he stabbed a guy in what looked like a drug deal gone wrong. A cold-blooded sniper shooting of two innocent kids? I just can't see it. He's not the type. He's hot-blooded; acts on instinct, and what would he have to gain anyway?"

I nodded. What Corbin had said matched my own thinking, but I wasn't about to let Rogan off the hook; not yet, anyway.

With that in mind, I reached for the computer and scrolled through Rogan's info.

I looked at my watch. It was eleven-forty-five. "Let's go see his parents," I said. "I want to make sure that gun isn't missing. We can grab something to eat on the way."

17

Monday afternoon, 1:15 p.m.

CHESTER ROGAN WAS THE KIND OF MAN YOU SEE IN Hardee's every Sunday morning, religiously, the way you see some people in church. Looking at him in suspenders and Velcro-fastened shoes, it was hard to imagine that he'd fathered someone like Nate Rogan. That is, until he scowled. The look was a twin to that of his son, and then it made sense.

"What do you want?" he asked, his eyes rheumy and red.

"I'm Captain Gazzara, Chattanooga PD," I replied, holding my badge up for him to see. "This is Sergeant Russell. We spoke to your son earlier. We'd like to ask you a couple of questions, if you have a moment."

"I don't," he snapped, closing the door.

I stuck my foot out and stopped it, dropping my polite smile.

"Mr. Rogan, you have two choices," I said. "You can talk to us here and now, or we can take you downtown and do it there. Which is it to be?"

He scowled again, revealing two rows of yellowing teeth, and opened the door again, but instead of inviting us in, he stepped out onto the porch and folded his arms.

"Well?" he snapped.

Out of the corner of my eye, I saw Corbin start to smile and then hide it. The situation was, I suppose, slightly humorous, but I didn't find it funny. I didn't want to be wasting my time or his. If his son wasn't our guy, I wanted to know and move on.

"Mr. Rogan," Corbin began, "we'd like to take a quick look at your son's rifle, the Winchester."

"What rifle? I don't know what you're talking about," he replied nastily.

"Your son told us that he used to own a Winchester 30-30 rifle, but he sold it to you before he went away. We'd like to see it."

"Tough shit. I don't have it."

Corbin and I exchanged a glance.

"Where is it?" I asked.

"I sold it," he said.

I frowned and said, "You sold it? I see. Then you have the paperwork, a bill of sale or a receipt from a dealer? I'd like to see it, please."

Those rheumy eyes turned shifty.

"I... no, I don't have it," he said, scowling. "Technically, it wasn't mine to sell, but we... I wanted it out of the house after... when they had Nathaniel."

Which meant that Nathaniel had probably had the gun illegally, and Chester got rid of it to cover for his son. But that 30-30 hadn't been the gun used in the assault that had put him away. It wasn't uncommon for people to purchase firearms from one another: neighbors or buddies. Well, in Tennessee, anyway. But it did create problems in situations like this one.

Without a bill of sale or a receipt, or anything to prove ownership had passed to someone else, we had only Nathaniel's word for it, which made me wonder if he still had it. And Chester couldn't prove that he'd sold it either.

"I sold that gun while he was in prison," Chester said in a rough voice as if reading my mind. "Going on twelve years or so now. My wife didn't like it in the house, so I got rid of it." He looked back and forth between Corbin and me, his bushy brows flipping up and down. "I'm telling you, my son doesn't have a gun no more. He can't even go duck hunting, can he? And y'all will never believe a word he says. You didn't then; you won't now."

I frowned. "What do you mean, 'didn't then'?"

"My boy stabbed that man in self-defense when that cracked-out hiker came at him," Chester said. "They said it was him that was cracked-out, that it was him that attacked the hiker. It wasn't true. It was the other way 'round. Damn lyin' police officers."

That didn't sit right with me. The man sounded sincere, and he was looking me right in the eye as he said it. People who lie don't do that.

And thinking back to seeing Nathaniel not much

more than an hour ago, it was true that prison dried many people out, but he didn't strike me as an addict. Addicts never really stop. I can usually tell, either by a nervous tic, a strange speech pattern, or extreme weight loss. But Nathaniel had nothing like that. He was articulate, built like a tank and looked healthy. But what Chester said was typical. They're all innocent, but there was something about Chester that had me thinking he believed what he was saying.

What if he was right? What if Nathaniel had just been defending himself, as he had every right to do? I shuddered to think that the man had done ten years for something he didn't do. But there was nothing I could do about that, but I did wonder if I should run it by the chief. It was never a good thing to go through cases like his again; the blowback from the departments concerned could be significant, but something was off about Nathaniel's situation.

I nodded, deep in thought. I was beginning to agree with Corbin that Nate Rogan wasn't our guy.

Corbin wrapped it up, politely. Chester didn't soften up much, but he did seem to get the impression that we were backing off, which was probably more than he expected.

We told him goodbye and left him standing on the porch, his arms still folded across his chest and a sour look on his face.

By then, it was almost two o'clock in the afternoon; time I was back in the office.

"So," I said, "we need to put Rogan on the back shelf for now. So where does that leave us?"

Corbin grunted, reaching a hand back to gently push Samson's curious nose away from his ear.

"A transient killer, maybe?"

I closed my eyes and let my head rest against the seat. "No... I'm not buying that," I said. "It just doesn't add up. You've seen the place. It had to be someone who knew their way around, and in the dark."

"Yeah. I suppose," he said reluctantly. "It would be difficult, in the dark and all."

He paused for a moment, then said, "Rogan, the son, he was angry when he saw who we were, but not the kind of angry that raises any red flags."

"Agreed."

"But he must have heard something, don't you think? Can you imagine how those shots must have echoed? But you know, he doesn't strike me as the spontaneous kind."

"Or a killer at all," I said.

"What if..." Corbin began, "what if... someone was angry about Caroline and Jared's relationship? An ex-boyfriend, maybe? After all, the family made it sound like he wasn't the most popular kid on the block. And love, and its derivatives, are all strong motives for murder: love, jealousy, hate, revenge."

I shook my head slowly. I'd already considered and partially dismissed it. "The method lacks passion," I said. "Most personal murders are done close up and messy. Such a killer likes to look his victim in the eyes and let him, or her, know why. This one was targeted, true, but from a distance. There would have been no satisfaction in it."

"I don't know then," he said. "It's a mystery to me. Sorry, Kate."

"Don't apologize," I said. "It's a mystery to me, too. Seven heads are always better than one, but so far we're all stuck."

But I knew the answers were out there somewhere. I just had to find them.

18

Tuesday morning, 1 a.m.

THE GLOW OF THE CELL PHONE LIT UP THE SKELETAL remains of my bedroom; a bed frame and mattress, and work clothes hanging from the closet door. Samson's bed in the corner, empty, since he was jammed in next to me.

I turned over and grabbed the phone. "Hello?" I snapped, my brain fighting to catch up with my body as I sat up.

"Captain Gazzara, this is Nina with dispatch. We need you to come in ASAP. There's been another attack."

I blinked once, and that was it; I was wide awake. Samson groaned but perked up as if he'd heard and understood the news.

I looked at the time. It was just after one in the morning.

"I'll go straight to the site," I said, voice sharp. "Where is it?"

"Just off highway 58 on a side road. I'll text you the exact coordinates. We already have officers out there securing the area. And, Captain Gazzara, there's a survivor."

"All right," I said as I jumped out of bed. "I'll be there as quick as I can. Contact Sergeant Russell and tell him to join me there."

"Will do," and with that, she hung up.

Me? I made a mad dash for the bathroom, took a quick shower, dressed and by one-thirty, Samson and I were out the door.

THE DRIVE to the scene was hectic despite the empty streets. I drove with my blue lights flashing and my yelper on, laying on the gas and taking corners a little too quickly for an SUV.

The crime scene was already lit up with red and blue lights and crawling with uniformed officers; most of them I recognized, but Corbin wasn't among them yet. In the backseat, Sammy, wearing his harness and badge, whined as I pulled in and put the SUV in park. He seemed to know that something was amiss.

A quick look at the GPS made my throat tighten. We might be right by the highway, but we were only two miles away from the cemetery. *It can't be a coincidence*, I thought as I attached Sammy's leash and let him out.

Another Ford SUV, similar to mine but wine-red, was parked by itself on a gravel pull-off. It was taped off and obviously the subject of the crime scene.

Two figures were silhouetted in one of the cruiser's lights. One was lying beside the vehicle with its arms spread. The other was Mike Willis.

Three steps toward the scene revealed that a dark substance around the body on the gravel was blood.

The SUV door was open, but there was no one inside. The survivor, I presumed, had already been taken away to the hospital.

Mike was carefully examining the vehicle. "Hey, Mike," I called over the sound of officers chatting and the noise of the occasional semi going by on the highway.

Willis looked around, blinking blearily at me; his shaved head glinted in the lights.

"Good to see you, Kate," he said tiredly and then caught himself. "Well... you know what I mean."

"Looks like you'll have more to work with on this one. No team tonight?"

He shook his head. "They'll be here soon."

At least it was a clear night. Not a cloud in the sky.

A short, round figure appeared from the other side of the SUV and I jumped, pressing a hand to my chest. "Geez, Doc. You scared the crap out of me."

Doc Sheddon chuckled. He looked just as exhausted as Willis. He turned serious; his face suddenly grim.

"Sorry, Kate," he said. "I didn't mean to scare you. I was taking a look at the driver's side. She survived, you know."

"Yes, I heard," I replied. "How's she doing?"

"She'll be fine," he said. "The bullet passed through her right bicep, here." He pointed to his own arm. "Lots of blood. She passed out. Lucky for her. Probably saved her from a second shot. Come take a look at the other victim."

Doc took me gently by the elbow and steered me toward the body on the ground.

He was lying on his back with his arms spread wide, obviously the result of the impact of the bullet. A young man in his mid to late teens. His eyes were open, and there was some light scruff on his chin and cheeks, more like a peach fuzz than an actual beard. And... there was a neat round hole in his forehead just above the right eye. Just a trickle of blood down and into his ear that belied the copious amount of blood on the ground.

"Through and through," I said, "judging by the amount of blood on the ground."

"Undoubtedly," Doc said.

"Time of death?" I asked.

"Now, Kate," he replied. "You know better than that."

"Oh, come on, Doc. Give me a hint, damn it."

"Somewhere between eleven-thirty last night and twelve-thirty this morning, I should think."

"Who found them?"

"We don't know," he said. "Probably a passing motorist. It's visible from the road. Someone called 911. Wouldn't give his name and hung up before we could get more details."

"Geez," I said. "That's a bummer. What time did he call it in?"

"Around midnight, so I'm told."

"So," I said, "what d'you think? Has our cemetery killer struck again, or what?"

"Definitely not what," he replied. "Definitely a rifle. Shot from a distance, through the windshield, both of them and, by looking at the wound in the boy's head, it could be a 30-30. The one that hit the girl went through the windshield, her arm, then the seat and is embedded in the door frame. Probably too damaged to get a match."

He paused for a second, looking down at the boy. "Too young," he said, shaking his head. "Between seventeen and nineteen, I should say. For this young man, one gunshot wound to the head. No bullet, of course. As far as we can tell, it passed through the windshield, his head and then out through the rear window, which accounts for the blood spatter on the passenger side. I doubt very much that Mike's people will find it, but you never know. Stranger things, Kate. Stranger things."

"The survivor?" I asked, looking at Doc but unable to see his eyes due to the glare on his glasses.

He sighed. "I didn't get that good of a look at her. You know mine is the world of the dead. She was already in the ambulance when I got here, but I did get a quick peek. I was looking at the driver's side where she was sitting when you arrived."

"So," I said. "If he was shot inside the car, what's he doing out here?"

"Ah," he said. "Thereby hangs the tale, as our good friend William Shakespeare said. The passenger-side door was open when Mike got here, so it had been opened by someone else. The boy's body is less than six feet away. Somebody dragged him out of there. But who? The driver, the person that called it in? Or... the killer?"

"Geez," I said for what must have been the fourth time.

"Indubitably, my dear Watson."

"Oh, stop it, Doc," I said. "Let me think, will you?"

"Both shots were aimed head-on, from over there, which means..."

"I know what it means," I said. "It means the crazy son of a bitch has struck again."

"Absolutely," he replied, nodding toward a thick clump of bushes on the north side of the field. I knew that somewhere beyond them was the cemetery where Caroline and Jared had died just four days earlier, and I shivered, and not from the cold.

"My guess is the boy was shot first, and the girl ducked and tried to cover her head. But that's just a guess. You'll talk to her at the hospital, I'm sure. Kate, not to be morbid, but it seems someone really doesn't like teenagers."

I laughed humorlessly, knowing that Doc didn't mean it as a joke. Because he was right; this was just too perfect. Two teens targeted, again, and I was wracking my brain for the *why*.

Why teens? Why couples? Why kill them like this?

I took one last look at the boy before turning and heading for McCarty, the same officer who'd been first at the cemetery scene.

"Doug," I greeted him, "the other victim?"

"She was transported to the hospital about ten

minutes before you got here. My guess is they're already there, and she's being treated."

I nodded absently, still trying to take in the situation. "A name?" I asked.

We were briefly interrupted by a dingy sedan pulling up and Aubrey Pugh stepping out with his camera in hand. He looked less than energetic as he picked his way through the scene to where Mike Willis was still working the passenger-side door.

Doug spoke quietly with another officer, a female, and the one, I was told, that initially responded to the dispatcher. He turned back to me and said, "Her name's Lindsey Waller, nineteen. Her parents have already been notified."

"Okay," I said. "Good. I'm going to hang around until the rest of my team arrives—" I broke off, seeing Corbin get out of his car. "Then Sergeant Russell and I will head for the hospital. You guys good here?"

Doug nodded. "Of course, Captain. This is not my first—"

"Don't say it, Doug," I said, smiling at him.

He nodded, smiled back at me and walked away.

Corbin joined me and said, "Cooper and Dani are on their way. You want to catch me up?"

I briefly filled him in on the details and then told him to follow me to the hospital. Which he did.

19

Tuesday morning, 3 a.m.

WE ARRIVED AT THE ERLANGER HOSPITAL emergency room at a little after three-thirty that Tuesday morning, which was, as it always is, busy.

"Sammy will be fine, right?" Corbin asked quietly as we checked in at the main desk with our IDs.

"Of course. I left him curled up on his bed."

"How can I help you?" the receptionist asked.

"I'm Captain Gazzara," I said, showing her my badge. "We're here to see a Lindsey Waller. She would have been brought in just after midnight."

She nodded. "Of course. She's in room 2214. Take the elevator to the second floor and follow the blue line."

"You going to be okay?" I asked, glancing at Corbin as we waited for the elevator. He looked tired. "It might be a long morning."

"Yeah, yeah, I'll be fine," he replied. "I've just gotta get rolling."

I knew exactly what he was thinking. The case was turning into a disaster. The killer had struck again, and we were still no further forward. Another family had lost a child.

"At least the girl is still alive," I muttered.

The receptionist must've made a call because a male nurse was waiting for us when the elevator doors opened.

"Captain Gazzara?" he asked.

I nodded and said, "Yes. This is Sergeant Russell."

"I'm Cam," he replied. "Nurse in charge. If you'll follow me, I'll take you to see Lindsey."

"How's she doing?" I asked.

He looked over his shoulder at me. "Fine. She lost a lot of blood, but she was lucky. I'll let Dr. Silva fill you in. She's the surgeon on call tonight. Here we go."

The door was open, but the light inside was dim. Cam stepped just inside the door and gestured for us to enter. The room was a double, but Lindsey was the only occupant. She was propped up in bed. Her eyes were closed. She looked pale and drawn. Her parents were seated at her side. When she heard Cam, she opened her eyes and looked at us.

"Hello, Lindsey, Mr. and Mrs. Waller," I said quietly. "I'm Captain Gazzara. This is Sergeant Russell. How are you doing, Lindsey?"

The girl looked at us, her eyes wide, glassy. She was wearing a hospital gown with the right sleeve rucked up around the shoulder, her upper arm wrapped in gauze and tape.

Lindsey's mother looked at us and smiled. She looked worn out.

"I'm Lindsey's mother, Marissa Waller," she said. "Can we talk outside?"

Cam stepped further into the room and said, "I'll stay with Lindsey."

I nodded, and Corbin and I stepped back out into the hallway, where we were quickly joined by the Wallers.

"Michael Waller," the girl's father said as he pulled the door shut behind him.

"It's nice to meet you both," I said, offering him my hand. "I only wish it was under better circumstances. I do need to talk to Lindsey, but before I do, I'd like to get some basic information from you."

The pair nodded wearily. "Of course," Mr. Waller said.

Corbin took out his notepad.

"How old is Lindsey?" I asked.

"She turned nineteen in April," Marissa said.

"And she lives at home with you?"

"Yes," she said. "She still lives with us, but she's planning to go to college next year—Alabama. She decided to take a year off to save some money and—"

"And spend a little time with her boyfriend, Daniel," Michael Waller said, interrupting her.

It was obvious from the looks on their faces that the boyfriend was the second victim.

"Daniel?" Corbin asked.

"Daniel Thomas," Michael replied.

"Did you know Lindsey was out tonight, and that she was with Daniel?" I asked.

"Yes," Marissa said. "Of course we did. He's a nice..." she paused, her mouth open. It was as if she'd just realized the boy was dead.

I nodded. She closed her mouth, shook her head and continued, "He was a nice boy. He was..." Again she shook her head, looked down at the floor. Her husband touched her arm. She nodded and continued, "Once she graduated, we eased up on Lindsey's curfew. She and Daniel stay out late a lot. *Stayed...* out."

"The Ford is Lindsey's," Michael said. "Dan's car is at our house. I think they just... drove around a lot. Talked, you know... and yes, they probably made out, too. I know we did, didn't we?" He took his wife's hand and squeezed it.

"And Daniel's parents," Corbin asked levelly, "they were okay with them being out late?"

The moment of hesitation spoke for itself.

"Not... exactly," Marissa said. "Lisa, Dan's mother, is very conservative and protective of him. That's partly why... Oh, dear Lord," she said, shaking her head. "Someone needs to tell Lisa."

"Don't you worry about that," I said. "I'm sure someone has already contacted Mr. and Mrs. Thomas." I wasn't sure, but now that we had a name, I could make sure someone would.

"D'you have a number for the Thomases?" Corbin asked.

Marissa gave it to him. He looked at me. I nodded, and he stepped away to make a call. He returned less than a minute later to say that they already knew; Mike Willis had found the boy's wallet and ID, and someone was on their way to inform his parents.

And me? All I could think of was that I was glad it wasn't me that had that awful task to perform.

By then, though, tears were running freely down Marissa's cheeks. She turned into her husband's arms, and Michael looked at us over the top of her head.

"I think you should know," he said quietly, "that Lisa wasn't exactly thrilled that Dan and Lindsey were dating."

Corbin frowned, his pen poised over his notepad.

"Why was that, do you think?" I asked.

"Well, for one thing, Dan's more than a year younger than Lindsey. He just turned eighteen, and he was supposed to graduate next year. Like Marissa said, Lisa is protective, and I think she thought Lindsey and Dan were becoming a little too attached to each other."

"Thank you," I said. "That's good to know." And it was. At some point I was going to have to talk to the Thomases, and I didn't want to run into a rant that Daniel's death was Lindsey's fault. I'd met people like Lisa Thomas before, and they're always quick to place the blame on someone else.

"Just a couple more things, and then we'll talk to Lindsey," I said. "Has she ever mentioned that she was having problems with anyone? A jealous ex-boyfriend, perhaps, or someone she didn't like?"

Marissa turned to me again, her eyes still watering. They both shook their heads.

"No," Marissa said. "Dan was her first real boyfriend; she got along with everyone. Dan was such a nice boy. I can't imagine anyone not liking him."

I nodded. "Why, d'you think, were they out there on Highway 58?"

Marissa shrugged but didn't reply.

"I've no idea," Michael replied. "Just riding around, I suppose."

"Well," I said. "That's enough for now, I think. If you don't mind, I'd like to talk to your daughter."

"Of course... Yes." Michael said. "You'll want to talk to her alone?"

"Yes," I said. "If you don't mind."

He nodded. "Of course. We'll wait out here. We haven't talked to her about... well, not much. She'll probably be more comfortable talking to you without us hovering around."

I thanked them for their understanding. Corbin and I stepped back into the room, closing the door behind us.

Corbin motioned to Cam that it was fine for him to stay. He nodded but said he had other patients and that if she needed him, she was to push the button on the bed at her side, and he left us alone. Corbin and I sat down, me closest to her.

She looked alert, though her face was pale, and she was obviously in pain.

As I introduced us, she winced and shifted herself, though she didn't complain.

Lindsey Waller was a pretty young thing—cute, in fact—with dark auburn hair, hazel eyes, full lips, and a full sleeve of tattoos on the uninjured arm.

"How are you holding up, Lindsey?" Corbin asked, smiling at her.

"I'm okay," she said, cradling her arm. "It doesn't hurt anymore; because of the meds, I guess. The blood scared me, though. I thought I was going to bleed to death."

"I'm sure you did," I said. "But you'll be fine."

Lindsey nodded, breathed deeply and sighed, laid her head back on the pillow and closed her eyes.

"Daniel's gone, hasn't he?" she said without opening them.

"I'm afraid so, yes," I said. "I'm sorry, Lindsey."

After a moment of silence, she opened her eyes, lifted her head and said, "The cops wouldn't tell me. They wouldn't tell me anything, but I knew; deep down, I knew. He was sitting next to me. They shot him right in the forehead. I got him out of the car, but he was too heavy and I only had one hand."

Corbin and I exchanged a look.

"Lindsey?" I asked.

"What I don't understand is why they just shot me in the arm. Why didn't they kill me, too? They only shot me in the arm," she said slowly, lifting the forearm of her injured limb off the bed, wincing as she did so. "I was sitting right next to him. They could have killed us both. Unless it was a lucky shot that killed Dan."

She started crying again, sniffling, turning away to

wipe her cheeks. I waited for her to compose herself, which took a minute or two.

"Lindsey," I said. "We need to know exactly what happened out there tonight. Tell us what happened. Start at the beginning."

"Yeah, well, we drove around for a bit. We went up on Signal Mountain to the overlook and parked. Mostly we just talked, you know? Dan... he liked to talk. He was very intelligent, you know? We kissed and made out some. Nothing like... well. Then we drove around for a while, and I don't know why we ended up on Highway 58, but... well, anyway, we got something to eat at Zaxby's." She smiled; her wet cheeks glistened in the harsh light. "Dan eats a lot. *Ate* a lot." Fresh tears rolled down her cheeks, but she was holding it together. She took a long, shuddering breath. "We were driving out to the marina to hang out for a bit before heading home."

"Island Cove?" Corbin asked.

Lindsey nodded. "Yeah. But something went wrong with the car," she said, frowning. "We didn't know what. It started juddering and jerking, like it was having a hard time. Dan told me to pull over, so I did. He said to wait, to let it cool down. He doesn't know anything about cars."

She closed her eyes tightly. Then opened them again and looked at me. "I wish I could take it all back. I shouldn't have pulled over. I should've just turned around and gone home. Poor Dan," she whimpered.

"Lindsey," I said, reaching out and taking her hand. "You mustn't blame yourself. There's nothing you could have done." I squeezed her hand, then released it.

"Then what happened?" I asked, hating that I had to make her relive it.

"I pulled off and we sat there for maybe ten minutes, and I was just about to start the engine again when there was this huge, loud crack and the windshield shattered... Well, not shattered, but sort of... I don't know. I thought at first a rock from a truck had hit it, you know. But when I looked at Dan... Then it happened again, and my arm was, like, wrenched backward. It didn't hurt at first, and then... oh my God, the pain. I panicked. I knew we'd been shot, and I thought we'd be shot again, so I jumped out and ran around the car. I got Dan's door open and dragged him out, but he was so heavy. And then I think I must have passed out. I seem to remember a car stopping, but... That's all I can remember until the ambulance and the cops came."

By then, she was staring straight ahead at the blank TV on the wall.

"He didn't even make a sound," she whispered.

"You said you think you remember a car stopping. Do you know what make it was?" I asked.

She shook her head.

"How about the color?"

"Silver, or white, maybe, and it was a truck, a pick-up." She frowned, thinking.

"Okay," I said. "You're doing fine, Lindsey. I want you to think hard before you answer this question. You say it was a truck and that it might have been white or silver. You didn't happen to notice the rear wheels, I suppose?"

She shook her head, frowned and said, "No. Why would I?"

Why would she indeed, I thought.

"Which direction was it coming from? Do you remember?" I asked.

She thought for a moment, then said, "It was coming south, from the other direction, I think, towards us."

I nodded. "Okay... okay. That's good. You're doing great. Just a few more questions. Did anyone get out of the truck?"

She hesitated and glanced at me.

"I don't remember anything like that," she said, "but I thought I saw someone while we were parked and waiting for the engine to cool down—before Dan was shot. I told him I did, but he said I was imagining things."

"Where?" I asked. "How far away?"

She heaved a deep breath and blew it out through her lips. "I don't know. It's hard to say. It was dark. It was just a shadow. Maybe I was imagining it."

"Try to remember, Lindsey," I said. "It's important."

Again, she breathed deeply, then said, "Up front and to the right, maybe... Oh, I don't know. Not far. Maybe twenty-five... thirty yards. There were some bushes there."

I nodded. Doc and I had noticed the bushes, too.

Is that where the shooter was? I wondered. *If so, did she see him?*

"Tell me what you saw, Lindsey. Was it a man? Did you see his face, his clothing, anything?"

"No, it was too dark and my headlights were off." She

screwed up her face and took a moment to think. "They were wearing a baseball cap. Yeah, that's it. It must have been a man. I only saw him for a second. He was there, and then he was gone. Oh, and he wasn't running. He was moving slowly. I'm sorry, Captain. That's all I can remember."

"Don't be sorry," I said. "You're doing great. Take a breath and relax. There's no hurry."

I let her lie for a moment, holding her arm, then she looked at me and said, "There's something else. The truck that stopped. It had a diesel engine."

"You're sure?" I asked, frowning. "What makes you think it was a diesel?"

"My dad drives one," she replied. "They make a particular noise. You know one when you hear one, don't you?"

She wasn't wrong. It was easy to recognize a diesel engine by the clatter it makes.

I looked at Corbin. He gave me a nod, indicating he had all the details. But, as I sat there looking at Lindsey, I knew we had little more to go on than we did when we walked in the door.

What *did* we have? We had a shadow that could have been a man wearing a ball cap and a diesel pickup truck —white, possibly silver—that might or might not be connected to the crimes. It wasn't much, but it was more than we had before. But it was nothing if we couldn't find a white or silver truck with dual rear wheels.

But Lindsey was right. Why didn't he kill her instead of just wounding her? He was obviously an expert shot.

He'd nailed Daniel in the forehead, in the dark. I figured he must have been using a night-vision sniper scope. They're easy enough to obtain, not like a suppressor. You need a special permit for one of those, and they're not easy to get.

"Lindsey, can you think of anyone who would want to hurt you or Daniel?"

She frowned, eyes narrowed as she considered. "Not really, no. I mean... Dan's dad is in prison, but not for anything too serious. He was a dealer, but a pretty low-level one. And Lisa, Dan's mother, divorced him years ago, so Dan never saw him." Her eyes widened and then she laughed humorlessly. "Lisa... though. Now there's someone who doesn't like me."

Lindsey rolled her eyes but was quick to add, "Not that she'd try to kill me or anything. I can't imagine her even touching a gun. Plus, the person I saw was too tall for sure."

"Were any of your friends out tonight?" Corbin asked. "Did you meet up with them?"

After a second, she shook her head. "Not that I know of, no. Monday night and all."

Was the father somehow connected? I doubted it, but we'd check his record.

"Wait," Lindsey said, "I do have an ex who's been kind of a jerk lately. We broke up about a year ago, right before I graduated, and I ran into him last week. He called me a slut." She muttered the last part, looking away from us with a heavy sigh. "Even though I didn't start dating Dan until after we'd been broken up for a while."

"His name?" I asked.

"Ben Whitt. He's my cousin's best friend. That's how I met him."

"What?" I said, suddenly on high alert.

"Ben Whitt?"

Holy... He's one of the rednecks that stopped by the cemetery scene.

"And your cousin, what's his name?"

"Luke Webber."

You've got to be kidding me.

20

Tuesday morning, 8:30 a.m.

IT WAS AFTER FIVE THAT MORNING WHEN CORBIN and I left the hospital, and by then we were both running on fumes, but it was *not* the time to slow down. We had a lead to run down. Well, it felt like a lead.

"I need to go home and shower and change clothes," I said, "and so do you. Let's meet up at the office around eight-thirty. That will give me time to get something to eat. Samson must think I've abandoned him. Oh, and by the way, I have a closing at noon, so I'll be out for at least a couple hours, okay?"

He nodded. "Sounds like a plan. See you at eight-thirty. You want me to gather the clan for you?"

"No. Not right away. I need to think first. I *will* get hold of Cooper, though, and have him and Dani go visit Nate Rogan. I want to know where he was last night and what kind of truck he's driving."

AND SO I WENT HOME, took a leisurely shower, made myself some scrambled eggs—the last three items in the refrigerator—and fed Sam, who was more than glad to see me. Then, at around ten after eight, I loaded him into my blue and white SUV and headed out along East Brainerd Road to I-75 and from there to Amnicola Highway and the police department.

It was just before eight-thirty when Sam and I exited the elevator, stepped into the situation room and headed to my office, stopping along the way to tell Cooper and Dani to join me in my office in fifteen minutes. I needed time to brew coffee and get my head in order. Two minutes later, Corbin knocked and stuck his head through the open door.

"Can I come in?" he asked.

"Sure," I replied. "Close the door behind you. You want some coffee?"

"No. I'm good."

I glanced at him, surprised. "Well, I do. Sit down. Cooper and Dani will be here in a minute. I'll get them sorted, then you and I will go and talk to Ben Whitt—and maybe Luke Webber, too. You had breakfast yet?"

He nodded. "I grabbed a sausage and egg biscuit from Hardee's on the way in. You?"

"Yup. Scrambled eggs at home—"

I was interrupted by a knock on the door. It opened and Cooper stuck his head in. "You ready for us?"

"Yes, come on in and take a seat," I said, then turned

to my coffee pot which was just finishing up. I poured myself a large mug of black and sat down behind my desk.

"Good morning," I said. "You two all right?"

They said they were, so I continued, "I need you to go to Nathaniel Rogan's place. I want to know where he was last night and if he has an alibi. I also want to know what kind of truck he drives, what color it is, and if it has dual rear wheels. He won't be happy to see you, but don't let him get to you."

Cooper had a hot temper and sometimes had trouble controlling it. "Keep it professional. I mean it, Cooper. Keep it together."

"Will do, Captain," he said, humbled.

"How's the victim, Captain?" Dani asked. "She doing okay?"

"Yes. She's badly shaken up and devastated by the death of her boyfriend, but she'll recover from the wound. The experience? It will haunt her for the rest of her life."

I paused, took a sip of coffee, looked at Dani, then Cooper and said, "Any questions? No? Good, then off you go. Keep in touch. Let me know how it goes."

They left, and Corbin and I spent a few minutes talking things over while I finished my coffee.

"All right," I said finally. "Let's do this. We'll take my SUV. All right, boy, let's get to it." And Sammy scrambled to his feet and went to the door.

Me? I was looking forward to getting eyes on Ben Whitt. It was just ten hours after the shooting, and if he'd been involved, I was pretty sure I'd be able to see it on him. My thinking was that there was no way a kid that young could be cold enough to hide the after-effects of shooting someone dead.

Hearing that Lindsey had dated Ben Whitt only a year ago had been a surprise, a lucky one, almost an afterthought. But was it too good to be true? Could the attack really be the work of a jealous ex-boyfriend? And if it was, how did it connect to the murders of Caroline and Jared? Were they just practicing for the real thing?

All of that was spinning around in my head as I drove across town on autopilot. My mind went back to the first time I'd seen Ben Whitt and Luke Webber that Saturday morning at the cemetery.

I'd shrugged them off as a couple of teen lookie-loos, rubbernecking the crime scene, which wasn't unusual. Ben Whitt had, for the most part, been polite, but was that a put-on? I remembered thinking that there was something about him I didn't like.

And, then, there was his buddy Luke. I remembered thinking that they were a couple of troublemakers; you know, typical, loud-mouthed country boys.

The Whitt home was on Kings Road, not more than a couple of miles or so from the cemetery and four from last night's attack.

I made a right onto a nice, but short, paved drive and pulled up in front of a large Cape Cod, surprisingly nice considering what I had imagined were rednecks living there. Obviously, I was wrong. But there, just to the left, was the red Ford F250 pickup, and it did not have dual rear wheels.

I put the SUV in park and rolled the window down.

"That look familiar?" Corbin said. "And look at the rear wheels."

"Yes. I see them," I replied, "but it's not a diesel." It was an observation that temporarily crushed my spirit. "Maybe she got it wrong."

And then, to the right, I noticed another vehicle, an older, beat-up truck, matte gray, light, and a diesel, but it didn't have dual rear wheels either. *Damn it!*

The door to *that* truck opened, and a man who looked to be in his early forties stepped out and walked toward us.

In the back seat, Sammy started growling. Corbin looked at him in surprise and then at me in question. I shrugged.

It was hard to blame Samson, though, because, at first glance, this guy was no winner. It was also hard to imagine that this house could belong to him. His prematurely graying hair was a mess. He was wearing a ratty T-shirt and had a cigarette hanging out of the corner of his mouth, and he was carrying a gun under his arm.

"Can I help you?" he called as he approached.

Samson's growls increased in volume. I tried to hush him as Corbin asked, "All good?"

"Yes. I think I'll leave him in the car."

Obviously. The last thing I needed was Samson biting some rich guy with *a gun*.

I assumed he was Ben Whitt's father and, trying not

to put too much focus on the gun, I was able to determine that it was a rifle. *What are the odds?* I wondered.

We both stepped out and closed the doors. I held up my badge, and Corbin introduced us.

"We'd like to have a word if you don't mind, sir," Corbin said.

"Chattanooga PD?" he said. "Sure. What d'you need?"

"What's your name, sir?" I asked, holding out a hand. He took it, not afraid to grip firmly, and met my eye.

"Kevin Whitt," he said with a smirk. "Nice to meet you, *Captain*. I'm surprised to see you out here, though." He looked at Corbin and then back at me. "Does this have to do with that mess up at the cemetery?"

Ben and Luke hadn't been lying the first time we'd run into them. The cemetery wasn't far from where he lived at all. And I didn't miss the stress Whitt had put on my title, either. He was, I figured, one of those good ol' boys who thought putting females in leadership positions was a joke. We were off to a great start.

"Indirectly, yes, it does. We're here to talk to your son. Ben."

Kevin Whitt's face turned a brighter shade of red. That he was shocked was evident, and I enjoyed wiping that smirk off his face.

"I... You want to talk to Ben? What for?" he asked angrily.

"Is he home?" I asked, ignoring the question.

"What d'you want with my son?" he asked, now on the defensive.

"We spoke to him on Saturday morning at the cemetery," Corbin said. "He was with his friend, Luke Webber. They stopped by on their way to the range. We just wanted to touch base with him again. Ask him a few more questions."

That Kevin Whitt didn't trust us was patently obvious, but he couldn't exactly say no without looking suspicious.

"Yeah, well... Okay," he said reluctantly. "Let me go wake him up. It's still a bit early."

After Mr. Whitt was out of earshot, I turned to Corbin and said, "See that gun?"

Corbin nodded and said, "Yes. It looks like a twenty-two. He probably uses it for squirrel hunting."

The front door opened again and Ben Whitt, followed by his father, stepped out onto the porch squinting in the bright light of morning. Wearing flip-flops and a sweatshirt and jeans, he looked just as scruffy as he did four days earlier.

"Hello, Ben," I said as he approached. "You probably remember us. I'm Captain Gazzara and this is Sergeant Russell. We have a few questions for you."

He glanced at his dad. He was short. Shorter than me by several inches, but he had the build of a football player, stocky, with wide shoulders, and he looked annoyed.

"D'you sleep in your clothes?" I asked. "That was pretty quick."

His face darkened and he shrugged. Kevin Whitt moved in close behind him.

"No," he replied. "I just didn't want to come out in my underwear, so I threw on my clothes from last night."

Ah, but Ben Whitt wasn't yet old enough to be a good liar. And, from the way his father was shifting from one foot to the other, he, too, knew his son was lying.

"Ben, do you own a 30-30 rifle?" Corbin asked.

Ben Whitt's dark eyes darted from Corbin to me and then back again. "Yes," he answered. "I hunt. I own several rifles, and handguns."

His answer wasn't unexpected. Tennessee is an outdoor state and many people hunt.

"You hunt what?" Corbin asked.

"Deer, duck, turkey, you name it. If it's in season, I hunt it," he said. "Squirrels. Raccoons when they're a problem."

He seemed nervous, and I wondered why.

"Is this about the cemetery or about squirrels?" Kevin Whitt asked, obviously irritated.

I held up a hand to appease him. "You're right," I said. "My apologies. Ben, where were you last night between eleven and one this morning?"

He frowned, eyes still bleary, so I added, "It doesn't look like you got much sleep. And I'd be surprised if you changed clothes that fast when your dad went and got you."

"Now, you listen here—" Mr. Whitt broke in, but I shut him up quickly.

"If we can't have this conversation here," I snapped, "I'd be happy to take him downtown and do it there. It's up to you."

He shut his mouth and glowered at me over his son's shoulder. Ben looked uneasy, and I knew we'd caught him out in another lie.

"I was here," he said. "Got back late, but I was here."

"What time?" Corbin asked.

"Round... eleven, maybe."

His dad nodded to confirm. "I was up watching TV and heard him come in. He was here all night."

I took another look at the red pickup. Saw the dirt on the tires. It looked fresh.

"Ben, we both know that's not true," I said carefully. "Where were you? What were you doing?"

"I'm tellin' you, he was here," Kevin Whitt said loudly, stepping around Ben. Corbin blocked him. Samson, in the back of the SUV, started barking loudly, and I wished I had him with me at my side. I had a feeling Kevin Whitt was a hothead, unpredictable.

But apparently the barking unsettled Ben. Either that or he knew we'd caught him in a lie, because he couldn't look me in the eye.

"Okay, so yeah," he said. "I went out again after I came home."

Kevin Whitt shut up, his mouth open as he stared at his son.

"Where did you go, Ben?" I asked. I was done playing around.

"Just out," he said, looking off into the distance. "Just... driving around."

"You can do better than that," I snapped.

"What's this all about?" Kevin asked. "Did something

happen last night? Is that why you're here?" He looked at Ben and said. "Don't say another word. You hear?"

I frowned, but Ben answered anyway. "I was out spotlighting."

My eyebrows rose, as did Corbin's. Not because he'd been hunting deer illegally, but because *that* had been his lie. But there had to be more...

"I didn't get anything," he said. "I went to a new spot, but there was nothing out, all right?"

"Is there anyone who can confirm that?" Corbin asked.

"No. I was on my own," he muttered.

"And you had your 30-30 with you?" Corbin said.

"We're going to need that rifle," I said, "for comparison."

This time, Kevin Whitt had it together when he interrupted. "Then you'll need a warrant," he snapped. "Darn it. It's supposed to be my day off. Ben, get your ass back in the house. Now!"

He dug his wallet out of his back pocket, aggressively flipping it open, took out a card and flipped it to Corbin who barely managed to catch it.

"If you have any reason to question him further, you can call my firm and make an appointment. This conversation is over. I want you to leave. Now."

I looked at Corbin. I was confused. So was Corbin. Whitt grabbed his son by the shoulder, spun him around, marched him back to the house and slammed the big fancy door, hard.

"Let me see that," I said, nodding at the card in Corbin's hand. He handed it to me.

I looked at it. It read, *Whitt, Low & Associates. Attorneys at Law. Kevin Whitt Esq. Managing partner.*

Kevin Whitt was a lawyer.

I actually laughed out loud at the absurdity of the situation.

"Well," I said. "That's about the last thing I expected."

"I know. But he's right... We need a warrant for the rifle, and we need to talk to him properly."

"You're right," I said. "We need to talk to him about his relationship with Lindsey. There's a lot here we're not seeing... Let's go drop in on his friend Luke Webber."

21

Tuesday morning, 9:45 a.m.

THE WEBBER RESIDENCE, THE EXACT OPPOSITE OF the Whitt's, was a double-wide mobile home on a small, wooded lot with a short, paved driveway pitted with potholes, and an overgrown yard, with a small patch of grass at the front in dire need of mowing. The grill, just to the left of the steps, rusted and missing a leg, was propped on a stack of cinderblocks. There was also a garage to the left and partially set back behind the mobile home. It looked to be almost as big as the home, and better kept. I figured it must be somebody's workshop. Parked just to the left of the garage sat an F-150 pickup. Yup, there's a lot of them in Tennessee.

As I pulled up, a mangy cat high-trailed it from beneath the three short stairs into the woods. In the back seat, Samson perked up.

At first, I thought it was the cat that had caught his

attention, but he started growling, his brown eyes fixed on the mobile home. *Okay,* I thought, *so maybe he'd had a bad experience with mobile homes.* Either that or he was sensing something else.

Corbin reached around and ruffled his fur. "What is it, fella?" he asked.

"Sheesh," I said. "I don't know. I still don't know that much about him. Sometimes he just amazes me. It's like he has some sort of intuition. I often wonder just who and what his previous master was. Maybe I should check his sheet and see." In truth, I should have done that weeks ago when I rescued him from the SWAT team. He'd been guarding his dead master's body, and they were about to shoot him when I stepped in. He took to me right away. Short story, right?

Again, I decided to leave him in my vehicle, and we stepped out onto the driveway.

I couldn't help but wonder if Lindsey Waller's home was anything like the Webber'. If so, she and Ben Whitt had had quite a "Romeo and Juliet" thing going when they were dating. It was hard to imagine that someone of Ben Whitt's background would rub elbows with the kid who grew up in a trailer, but then, it's not entirely uncommon. People were brought together by all sorts of situations, especially high school. *And what about Luke and Ben? What kind of connection do they have?* I wondered.

One that Luke could fill us in on, I was sure. But would he? I really wanted to hear more about who Ben *really* was.

Corbin and I stepped up to the door, and just as I raised a hand to knock, it opened. Luke Webber stood before us, grinning widely.

He was my height, with sandy-blond hair, shaggy, falling over his eyes. He raised a hand and swept it back.

"'Morning, y'all," he said brightly. "I'm sorry, miss. I seen you out at the cemetery, but I don't remember your name."

"It's Captain Gazzara," I replied dryly, recalling the way the two of them had smirked at my title only a few days ago. "And this is Sergeant Russell. You heading out somewhere, Luke?"

His smile didn't fade at all. He seemed to be taking our impromptu visit in stride. "Yes, ma'am, Miss Gazzara."

"Captain," Corbin said. Luke's smile wavered a little, but he continued to look at me instead of Corbin.

"Where are you going?" I asked casually.

"I'm heading out for work. I have a few minutes, though, if you need to talk."

I nodded, and Corbin took over. "Where do you work, Mr. Webber?"

Luke seemed to find the title, Mr., funny as his grin widened. "I work for the Dzen Company, sir. Sergeant," he corrected himself. "Construction." He held up his fist, clutching a reflective jacket. "Though mostly we're doin' roofin' this time of year. We do a little bit of everything at Dzen."

At this point, the constant smile was becoming irritating, but I tried not to show it and said, "Well, if you do have a few minutes—"

Luke half-turned, gesturing inside. "Sure. Come on in. There's still coffee on."

"Thank you," I replied. "I'm good." I had no intention of taking him up on the coffee. I could have used some, but I wanted to stay sharp and keep boundaries solid.

The mobile home was clean and tidy, though somewhat bare. The carpeting was gray and worn, the wallpaper light blue and white, with songbirds dotted here and there. And finally, the valence curtains over the kitchen sink gave away a woman's touch.

"Nice place you have here," I said genuinely, speaking quietly in case anyone else was home.

"Ah, well, thank you, ma'am, but I cain't take no credit for that. It's all my mom. She... was a nurse." He smiled again, a dimple showing on his left cheek.

"Do you mind?" I asked, moving toward the small kitchenette.

He shook his head and said, "Be my guest. Sit yo'selves down."

I sat down at the table. Corbin joined me, his face unreadable, and I wondered if he found Luke as charming as he seemed to be.

"Luke," Corbin said as he, Luke, sat down, "we're here to talk about your friend, Ben Whitt. How long have you known him?"

Ah, there it was. The smile dropped. and I got a glimpse of intelligence in his eyes and then it disappeared, masked by confusion.

"This is about Ben? I've known him since we was in junior high. Why? Is he okay? He in trouble?"

I shook my head. "No. But we spoke to him a little while ago, and we just need to confirm some of what he said."

"Okay..."

His reaction seemed genuine, and I wondered if Ben had called him. It would be the teenager thing to do.

"We know Ben was out last night, Luke," Corbin said. "Were you with him?"

"Well, yeah. We went to get burgers at Red Robin, hung out there until... Oh, I don't know, probly right about closing."

"Okay. Did you go anywhere after that?"

He shook his head slowly. "No... just drove around, mostly, ma'am."

"Drove around where?"

This time, we got a shrug, the confusion still lingering in his eyes. "Just around downtown. Cruising, mostly, not... anywhere particular. Is Ben okay?"

"Ben's fine," Corbin said. "You guys were in his truck, right?"

"Yeah. He picked me up. Dropped me back off after..."

His nerves were getting to him. He knew something was up, just not what, and I was pretty sure Ben Whitt hadn't called or texted him.

"Do you know where Ben went after he dropped you off?" I asked, watching his eyes.

"No." He shrugged. "Home, I guess."

"What time was that?" Corbin asked.

"About elevenish, I 'spose."

"He told us he went home," I said, "but he also said he went out again. Did he tell you anything about that?"

"No, ma'am. I'm sorry." The apology seemed genuine as he leaned toward us, hands balled around the reflective jacket in his lap.

"Have you and Ben ever gone spotlighting?" Corbin asked passively. That was the key because spotlighting deer was illegal in Tennessee, but it was also a practice that the young hunters loved.

Luke swallowed and slowly rolled his shoulders. "Might've checked it out," he replied, "seen what it was all about, but not recently, no."

"So you weren't out spotlighting with him last night?"

He shook his head emphatically, frowning. "He told you he was out spotlighting last night?" he asked. "That's... That's frickin' crazy. Why would he tell you that? He'll get his ass locked up."

He seemed genuinely shocked that his friend would admit to it.

"What can you tell us about Ben and Lindsey?"

Luke's eyes darkened as he looked back and forth between us. "What about Lindsey?" he asked quickly, voice low. "Ben has nothing to do with her."

"They dated. Isn't that right?" Corbin asked.

"Yeah, but... that was last year. A while back."

"You introduced them, didn't you?" I asked.

Now he looked annoyed, nodding slowly. "Yeah. We all go to school together, but yeah. Sometimes Lindsey would stop and say hi in the parking lot. That's how they got... talking."

"Did it bother you that Ben and Lindsey were dating?" He opened his mouth, shut it, then said, "I mean, it was like... weird, but Ben didn't mistreat her or anything like that. Is that why you're here? Did Lindsey say something about Ben?"

"Lindsey had an accident last night," I said. "We're here trying to find out what happened."

"Is she okay?" he asked, half-out of his seat, the jacket discarded on the floor.

I glanced at Corbin. He was watching him closely, frowning.

I was getting mixed signals, too. Luke Webber was like a rollercoaster. Charismatic, charming, then resentful.

"Lindsey's fine," I said. "You've known Ben for a long time, I take it?"

He nodded.

"How did he take it when Lindsey broke up with him? Was he upset?"

Sullen now, Luke licked his teeth and stared at me across the table. "No. The breakup was rough, but Ben knows..."

He broke off. *Ben knows. What does Ben know? That Luke wouldn't stand for it if he tried anything with Lindsey?*

"You said she's okay?" he asked.

"She's fine," Corbin confirmed.

I decided to give him a push.

"The thing about kids like Ben," I said, "kids from wealthy families. They tend to get whatever they want. Is Ben like that? Would he hurt Lindsey, d'you think? You know. Payback."

"He's not that stupid," he snapped. "He knows his place."

Knows his place? What does that mean?

"Look," he said. "I don't know what you think he did, but he didn't do it. Ben's a jerk, but he's harmless. He's all talk, like a lot of guys. Are we done here? I need to go to work, and I need to call my aunt. Is there anything else you have to ask?"

He stood up and grabbed his jacket.

"No," I replied as I stood up. "That's all for now, but we may need to talk to you again. Thank you for your cooperation."

He nodded, then led us to the front door and followed us out. We waited as he locked up. He glanced at us, then turned away and walked to his truck.

We walked slowly back to my car, watching as he pulled out of the drive, wheels squealing on the pavement as he made a hard left.

"What do you think?" I said.

"I don't really know... He seems like a polite kid. Defensive of his friend, which is normal. But it was weird, right? How quickly he got upset?"

"Yes," I said, reaching for the door handle. "I was expecting him to be more upset about his cousin being hurt, but..."

"He was more concerned about Whitt," Corbin said. "It felt, I dunno, misdirected?"

"Yeah. Exactly. I don't know, though. Maybe that's just how kids are these days? It takes them a while to process things."

Corbin grinned. "You're showing your age, Cap. Webber's no kid. He's twenty-one. I can't even remember what that was like. But you're probably right. He's probably just confused."

"You know," I said as I pushed the starter button, "something's bothering me. Why would someone kill her boyfriend and not her? Twenty-five yards... It was an easy shot, even in the dark, if he was using a night scope, and he's obviously a marksman. Why didn't he kill Lindsey? He had plenty of time. Was it just a coincidence that Whitt went out again, unaccompanied and unseen? I don't think so. I don't believe in coincidences, especially in cases like this. Spotlighting? Hah, I don't think so. We need to know more about Ben Whitt."

22

Tuesday morning, 10:40 a.m.

AFTER A MUCH-NEEDED BREAK FOR A LATE breakfast and coffee, Corbin and I were in my office at the conference table. I had my boots kicked up on an empty chair, sipping on a large cup of black coffee and Corbin was slouched back in his chair, staring blankly at his half-eaten egg burrito.

"You okay?" I asked. He was looking a little haggard.

"I'm good," he said, taking another bite while Samson waited patiently at his side for any crumbs to fall. Only moments before he'd had his big head in my lap.

"Cooper and Dani should be here soon," I said after a quick look at my phone, recalling my conversation with Chief Johnston. It hadn't gone well.

"Another one," he'd said. "This isn't going to play well with the press, Kate. What are you doing about it?"

"I'm on it, Chief. We're already making the rounds."

"Making the rounds? What the hell does that mean? There's a damn sniper out there killing kids, and you're 'making the rounds'? You're going to have to do better than that."

And so it went on; him asking questions I couldn't answer and me not wanting to tell him that we were at a standstill.

I told him about Ben Whitt, but I also told him I had no proof; nothing to tie him to either of the two attacks, and I needed a warrant for his 30-30 and to bring him in for a more detailed questioning. I also told him about Kevin Whitt and playing hardball with him wouldn't be easy. And it wouldn't. I'd already checked in with Jeanine in legal, and she'd told me that Whitt and company was, in fact, a "good ol' boy" firm with an impressive track record and were known for being ruthless. I told the chief we'd be lucky if we ever set eyes on Ben Whitt again, and that didn't go down well either. His final words before he hung up were, "Get it done, Gazzara, and quickly." He hardly ever called me Gazzara; only when he was truly pissed off.

Dani and Cooper arrived looking... tired.

"Good morning," I said, taking my feet off the chair. "Everything all right?"

Cooper said, "Yup. Why d'you ask?"

Dani sat down next to me and made a face.

"Just checking," I said. "You guys checked in with Nate Rogan, right?"

"We did," Dani said. She looked serious, focused.

"And?" I said. "How'd that conversation go?"

They exchanged a look. Cooper swallowed, then leaned forward and said, "He looked like he'd just gotten home."

"Well," Dani said, glancing at Cooper. "He seemed bothered; upset about something. We asked him where he was when those kids were attacked, and he said he was out coon hunting."

"And you believe him?" Corbin asked, blinking wearily.

Dani shrugged. "Yes. Actually, I do believe him." She glanced at me, almost as if she was apologizing.

I raised my eyebrows. "It sounds like too much of a coincidence, Dani. And I don't like those. They're too convenient."

"Yeah, me too... usually. Look, I know he's an ex-con, but my gut's telling me it wasn't him." She shrugged and said, "Sorry."

"Don't be sorry," I said. "In this job, we have to rely on our gut, a lot."

I let what she said sink in. But the fact that Nathaniel had been out when the kids were attacked was intriguing.

"Wait a minute," I said. "Coon hunting? Rogan isn't supposed to own a gun."

Dani and Cooper exchanged a look. "He doesn't have one," Cooper said slowly. "And I didn't see one. And anyway, Dani asked him about that."

She blushed, and I wondered if they didn't have something going on between them. Lord save us.

"And his answer?" I asked.

"He said he was with his friend, Gabe Corewall, and

Gabe had the gun. A twenty-two. Nate took his dogs and did the tracking."

"Okay," I said, then sat back in my chair. It wasn't even noon and I was already dead on my feet, or off my feet.

"Right," I said, gathering myself together. "Well, you know what to do. Take a break, hydrate, then check with Gabe Corewall and confirm Rogan's alibi, get eyes on the gun and—heck, yes—get eyes on any raccoons if they actually got any. I want all bases covered, got it?"

They both nodded, but then Cooper said, "Captain, no offense, but if you think Rogan's good for it, why not just bring him in and put the screws to him?"

Because I don't think Rogan's good for it.

"Just cause he's an ex-con doesn't mean he doesn't deserve the benefit of the doubt," Dani said reproachfully, frowning at Cooper.

Cooper muttered, "Yeah, right," and stood up.

"Hey," I said as Dani opened the door to leave. "Stay in touch. If you find anything, I want to know, soonest."

Cooper nodded and pulled the door closed behind him. I stood up and walked to my desk.

"What d'you think?" Corbin asked.

"I think I need to get some air," I answered. "I'll be back. Samson, you're in charge."

The shepherd was already passed out on his dog bed, having given up on the crumbs. I headed out into the situation room.

If it isn't Rogan, could it be Whitt? I wondered, frustrated.

23

Tuesday morning, 11:20 a.m.

IT WASN'T LONG AFTER DANI AND COOPER LEFT
that Jack, Hawk and Robar entered my office. They all
looked the worse for wear, though I was sure they'd
gotten more sleep than Corbin and I had.

"Good morning," I said, looking up from the report I
was writing of our conversation with Luke Webber.
"Take a seat. What've you got for me?"

The trio joined Corbin at the table, seemingly glad to
take a load off.

"I think we can rule out a cult," Jack said, leaning
back in his chair.

"I agree," I said. "This is looking more and more like a
one-man job. How'd the canvassing go?"

Jack shrugged, shook his head and said, "Me?
Nothing new."

"We found a neighbor who said he heard gunshots," Hawk said.

"Oh, yes?" I said, suddenly interested. "Where? What area?"

"The guy lives on Mimosa Circle."

"That's just off 58," Corbin said. "You think it was the attack on Lindsey and Daniel they heard? What time did they hear them, and how many?"

"Two shots," Anne replied. "As to the time, they weren't really sure. It was an older man and his wife. They said they thought it must have been sometime around eleven thirty or so, but neither of them bothered to check."

"Well, that fits," I said, leaning back in my chair and linking my fingers together behind my neck.

"About the same time as the first shootings, right?"

"Exactly," I said. "Or it could have been Ben Whitt illegally hunting deer," I said dryly, though I found it hard to believe a country boy like Whitt could have completely missed a deer frozen in the beams of his headlights.

"So, to play devil's advocate," Hawk said with a little grin, "before we completely cut out anything... weird... it's also around the same time that we know Jasmine Hall and Brad Herbert do their moonlight rituals, right?"

"I'm not ruling them out," I said. "Not yet, anyway. Jasmine struck me as the real deal. I did a little checking. It seems that witchcraft and the Wiccan lifestyle are making something of a comeback. Her buddy, Herbert, though, does seem to have an unhealthy interest in the cycle of life and... death."

"You're right," Corbin said. "It might be worth checking in on them again, Captain. Find out what they were up to last night. If we can place them in the area..."

"It would complicate things," I said thoughtfully, leaning forward. "I don't know. What do we have? Rogan? Dani doesn't think it's him, though he was out all night coon hunting with a friend. They've gone to check that out. And Ben Whitt, who has an alibi, tenuous at best, and a hot-shot lawyer for a father. Jasmine Hall and Brad Herbert are a strange couple. That's for sure, but do they have it in them to kill? I can't quite get my head around that. Let's say Caroline Davis had been interested in witchcraft or whatever Jasmine was up to. Why would they want to kill her? There's no motive that I can see. None of them have motives. And even if they did kill the kids in the cemetery, why would they go after Lindsey and Dan? It makes no sense. Nothing makes sense, damn it!"

"We'll go and check them out," Anne said, shaking her head.

Jack nodded, then he shook his head. "I have a date with Doc for Daniel Thomas's autopsy."

"Good," I said. "I suggest you get some coffee in you. I need you on your toes, Jack. Take notes, get them back to me, and then head home and get some rest. Hawk, Anne. Let me know how it goes."

I looked at my watch, then at Corbin and said, "Hey.

I have to go. I have to meet my realtor at noon—in less than twenty minutes."

———————

BENJAMIN POPPED out of the attached garage, waving enthusiastically. "Hi! You made it!" He jogged toward my SUV. I got out and opened the rear door, and he wrinkled his nose as Samson jumped out. Benjamin wasn't exactly a dog person. "Oh. Hi, Samson! You look so... handsome."

I smirked at his attempt to be polite, which failed miserably. He put up with Sammy sniffing his trousers for a moment and then gave him a wide berth.

The house was... cute.

I'd never been able to picture myself in a suburban neighborhood, but as I looked around the cul-de-sac, something came over me; I was excited.

I walked toward the house, keeping a close eye on Samson as he checked out the hedges on either side of the front steps. It was a Cape Cod, not too big and not too small, a pretty forest-green color with white window shutters that gave it a bit of a pop.

In the front yard, a pretty willow swooped down over the front of the drive, giving a sense of privacy. The back yard was fenced in with a tall wooden privacy fence.

Benjamin headed back to the garage, gesturing for me to follow. It was a single-car garage, but that was really all I needed. I'd probably be using it for storage anyway. Samson loped enthusiastically into the space, sniffing the corners and grinning up at the still slightly nervous realtor.

"So, they cleared out whatever they had in here. Left you a few buckets of paint." He tipped one of the paint cans toward me so I could see the writing scrawled on top: *Kitchen, Living Room, Upstairs Bath.*

Otherwise, the space was neat and clean. The concrete floor had been swept and a window on the back wall looked out onto the yard.

It was all hitting me now: this was my house. I *owned* it.

Seeing the look on my face, Ben grinned and handed me a set of keys. Two copies. "Ready to go inside?" he asked, hand on the doorway that would lead into the house itself.

I nodded and followed him into a small mudroom with tiled floors leading into the combined kitchen and dining area. The rooms smelled of cleaning products, but that was fine. When I actually moved in—maybe sometime this weekend, if I was lucky—I'd open the windows and air it all out.

Samson trotted from room to room, his tongue lolling out of his mouth. I couldn't help smiling as he explored. Benjamin chatted away as we did the walkthrough. I'd seen it once before. A small living room and a guest bedroom downstairs, with French doors leading to the back yard. A half-bath. Upstairs, the master bedroom with an attached full bath and another smaller bedroom. More space than I needed, really, or had ever had before.

What would I do with it all?

"I'm going to check out the porch and make sure they replaced that railing," Benjamin called from downstairs.

Samson and I stood at the top of the stairway. "Well," I said, "what do you think, Sammyo? We going to be okay here?"

He wagged his tail.

I nodded and took a deep breath before heading down to join Benjamin in the quarter-acre back yard.

I was truly excited, especially when you consider I'd been dealing with so many heartbreaking endings recently.

24

Tuesday afternoon, 3:45 p.m.

WHEN I ARRIVED BACK FROM MY CLOSING, I FOUND
Corbin still in my office and a uniformed officer at the
door.

"Ah, Captain," she said. "There's a Lisa Thomas here
to see you. You want me to show her in?"

I thought for a moment, remembering that Chief
Johnston had broken the news of her son's death to her
personally.

"Yes, please, Beth," I replied. "See if there's a vacant
interview room. We'll be there in a minute. I need a refill
first," I said, grabbing my empty mug.

"How'd it go?" Corbin asked.

"Like clockwork," I said. "We'll be in our new home
hopefully by the end of the week."

"Congratulations," he replied. "You want me to join
you in the interview room?"

"Yes. Why not? Two heads and that good stuff, right?" I said, feeling better than I had in a long while, though I still had a spree killer to catch.

Lisa Thomas appeared to be... gentle, forlorn, I suppose. She was seated at the interview table with her hands in her lap, her blonde hair up in an untidy bun and her cornflower blue eyes red and puffy. She wasn't exactly beautiful, but she was pretty, and I had a hard time relating to what Lindsey Waller and her parents had said about her being mean and disapproving of her relationship with her son.

"Mrs. Thomas," I said and introduced myself and Corbin. "Thank you for coming in. I know this must be a hard time for you."

"Daniel was my only son," she sniffed, wiping at her nose with a handkerchief. "The only good thing his father ever gave me." She said it with the bitterness of a battered woman, which probably explained some things; in particular, why she was so protective of her son.

"We're sorry for your loss, ma'am," Corbin said. "We're doing all we can to find the person who did this."

Those cornflower blue eyes flashed. "I know who did it," she declared, taking us by surprise.

"Oh?" I said. "And who would that be?"

"Those Wallers and Webbers," she spit out. "The whole family is full of crazies."

"O...kay," I said, then took a breath and continued, "Mrs. Thomas, we *are* aware that you weren't happy about your son's relationship with Lindsey—"

"*Relationship?* That girl was older than Daniel. She

took advantage of him. She distracted him; took him away from his responsibilities."

That seemed like a bit of a stretch. There was only a year difference between Lindsey and Daniel.

"And if he hadn't been seeing her—in the middle of the night, no less—he'd still be alive." She choked on the last word and began to cry.

She was right in that respect, but that was life. People are always finding themselves in the wrong place at the wrong time. There but for the grace of God, and all that stuff. Daniel's death wasn't Lindsey's fault, but Lisa Thomas would never see it any other way. She needed to blame someone, and Lindsey would do just fine.

"Why don't you tell us what your beef with the Wallers and Webbers is?" Corbin asked slowly, obviously trying to be careful how he phrased the question.

She sniffed, glanced up at him and tucked her hand-kerchief back into her lap.

"We've known them for quite some time," she said, her distaste evident. "My ex-husband was involved with them. That's how he got into the drugs, the fighting." Her lip curled as she spoke. "They're not good people."

While that piqued my interest somewhat, it wasn't exactly helpful. Though it did beg the question: were drugs involved in both killings?

"That's quite an accusation," I said. "D'you have anything to back it up?"

She looked at me with a flash of annoyance. And already, I was beginning to doubt the validity of what she was saying.

She stuttered for a moment and then said, "They're just bad people. They have all kinds of... stuff around. In their trailers, you know?"

From that, though we hadn't seen where the Wallers lived, I was pretty sure it, too, like the Webber's, was a mobile home.

"You're talking about mobile homes," I said.

She nodded, kneading the handkerchief between her fingers in her lap.

"Was your husband a user or a dealer?" I asked.

Her face twisted in an ugly way. My first impression of her as a sweet, grieving mother was quickly disappearing, and I found myself annoyed.

"I told you," Lisa Thomas said through gritted teeth. "They're *bad people*. Don't you think it's a little too convenient that Lindsey Waller was only shot in the arm? Don't you think that means she had something to do with this?"

Now that was way out there on a limb, and I barely caught myself from laughing out loud. Corbin raised his eyebrows so high they disappeared into his hairline, which is really saying something since he's prematurely balding. It was obvious that Lisa Thomas really had it in for Lindsey, and her extended family.

But you know, I did think it odd that Lindsey had managed to escape with only a bullet wound. One that had been serious enough to require surgery, yes, but still. How had the gunman—who, judging from the already three killing shots, was an expert marksman—only wounded the young woman? Had Lindsey just been lucky? There was no way to know. Nor did I really care. Not then, anyway.

"Mrs. Thomas," Corbin said. "We've already spoken with Lindsey and her family—"

"Have you spoken to the Webbers?" she snapped, interrupting him.

"Yes, we have," I replied. "And that's all I can tell you. We're doing everything we can to find Daniel's killer."

She sat back in her chair, her arms crossed over her floral-patterned dress, her bun beginning to fall, wisps of hair floating down around her ears.

"If you ask me," she said. "Lindsey Waller shot Daniel and then shot herself."

I stared at her. She was obviously upset, grieving, and maybe a little crazy.

"Mrs. Thomas," I said. "That's not possible. They were both shot at long range, with a rifle. Look, I suggest you go home and be with your family or friends."

"I don't have anyone else," she said, looking down at the table and bursting into tears. "It was just Daniel and me." She sobbed.

I looked at her, biting my bottom lip. At that moment, my heart ached for her. But it was a confusing mix of emotions that she stirred in me. But I steeled myself. I had to. I had to see her for what she was. Her wild accusations and her bitterness would do nothing to help us find her son's killer.

"I'll see you out," Corbin said, standing, effectively

ending the interview. "As soon as we know something, we'll be in touch. You'll be the first to know."

Me? I went back to my office, closed the door, leaned my back against it and closed my eyes, trying to decompress. Samson lifted his head, tilted it to one side and looked at me questioningly.

"It's a mess, Sammy," I said. "Who killed Caroline, Jared and Daniel and wounded Lindsey?"

The shepherd stared at me as if I'd lost my mind.

"Yeah, I don't know either," I said dolefully.

I looked at my watch. It was just after five. I'd been on my feet, so to speak, for more than seventeen hours and, very suddenly, it hit me: exhaustion. I'd been going almost nonstop since six o'clock on Saturday morning; four days straight, and I was truly bushed. I could do no more. Not without sleep. So I told Corbin to hold the fort and that I'd see him at eight the following morning, and I went home and crashed. I turned off my phone and slept eleven hours straight, from seven until six. And, by God, I think I deserved it.

25

I made it in to work that following morning—a Wednesday—just before eight to find Jack North already waiting for me.

"You have a second, Cap?" he asked as he joined Sam and me as we walked across the situation room, a folder in his hand.

"Yeah, of course," I replied. "Come on."

As he walked, he filled me in. "Ballistics matched the bullet from the cemetery to a 30-30, most probably a Henry. They found the remains of another in the frame in the back of the Waller girl's Ford. It was an impressive shot that killed the boy, Cap. Him and the two at the cemetery. Expert, I'd say."

Which made it all the more suspicious that Lindsey got off with just a wound, serious as it was.

I closed the door behind us, and Samson went to his bed.

"Doc said Daniel Thomas died instantly," Jack said. "The entrance wound was half an inch above the orbital socket. Punched right through his brain."

"Well, that's something, I suppose," I said, "that he felt nothing. I wonder though..." I paused for a moment. "Do they really feel nothing?" I shook my head. There was no way to answer that eternal question, so I turned the conversation to the gun.

"A Henry, huh?" I said. "A beautiful weapon, lever action. How many of those are there in Chattanooga, I wonder? It's going to take months to work through that list, and that's just the legal weapons. Geez, we need a break, Jack."

Jack snorted. "Yeah, months."

"Did Doc have anything to say about Lindsey's wound?"

"Yeah. Dr. Silva sent over a copy of her report. She got off lucky; no major blood vessels were hit, bones all intact. They had a pretty big exit wound to deal with, though. She went home late last night."

That made me feel better. I was glad for her that nothing had been broken. A wound from a 30-30 could be devastating. Jack was right; she got off lucky.

And it was at that moment that Chief Johnston, as if he'd sensed a moment of vulnerability, appeared in my doorway.

"Detective North," he said curtly, nodding at him.

Then he turned to me and said, "Kate. When you two are done here, come find me. We need to talk."

I nodded with a tight smile, already not liking where it was heading.

I was actually kind of surprised that he hadn't called me into his office before. He must have known that I was making little progress. I figured it was about time for me to face the music.

"We good?" I asked North as soon as we were alone once more.

He nodded. "Yup. I'll just finish this up and put the file on your desk. Let me know if you need anything, Cap."

He left, and I sat down, wishing I could have talked to Anne and Hawk before meeting with the chief, but it wasn't to be. I'd catch up with them later, along with Dani and Cooper. And, thank the Lord, Tracy Ramirez was due back from her vacation the next day, Thursday. It would be interesting, I thought, to see how Cooper took the return of his partner. He and Ramirez were close, but he was obviously very fond of Dani... which could complicate my plans to add her to the team when Hawk finally stepped down and retired.

"Come on, Sammy," I said. "We've got places to be and the chief to see. Try to turn those sweet eyes on him and soften him up a bit for me, okay?"

Again, he gave me that look that seemed to say, "Are you crazy, or what?"

26

Wednesday morning, 8:30 a.m.

Chief Johnston didn't waste any time in getting straight to the point. As soon as I shut his office door, he looked up and said, "Kate, the press is all over me. We need some sort of break in this case. We needed it yesterday. Sit down. Let's talk."

And so I did. I sat down across from him. "I know, Chief. It's a bear. I have several suspects, but I can't tie any of them to it. I'm working on it. You know that. I always do. It may take a while, but I'll get there."

He nodded. "I know you will. I have every confidence in you and your team. But the pressure's mounting. I've already had a call from the mayor this morning, and that woman from Channel 7 is all over it."

"At least you don't have Amanda Starke on your case," I said, trying to lighten things up a bit.

"Not funny, Kate," he said. "Corbin updated me

yesterday evening, after you'd gone home." He glared at me over his half-glasses.

"Oh, come on, Chief. I'd been working four days straight. I needed sleep. I'm no good when I'm half dead, you know that."

He nodded. "That I do. What about this witch woman, Jasmine Hall, and Brad Herbert? I also know you and Corbin went and spoke with an ex-con. Is there anything there?"

"Nathaniel Rogan," I said. "Yes, we talked to him."

"But you don't think he's good for it?" Johnston said, making it obvious by the look on his face that *he* thought Rogan was good for it.

"An ex-con living right near both crime scenes," he said. "Prior owner of the same type of gun—"

"Half the population of Hamilton owns a Henry 30-30," I interrupted, wincing as soon as I said it, but he didn't seem to notice.

"Kate, it seems to me you've had Rogan served to you on a silver platter, and you're trying to find a way to excuse all these *coincidences* with him."

"No! I'm not," I said. "We need to do our due diligence. Rogan has an alibi for the second event, and Dani and Cooper are following up on it. They're supposed to be reporting to me later today."

"Are you looking into anyone else?" Johnston asked, seeming to relax a little.

"We are," I replied. "Ben Whitt, but it's iffy."

"Whitt? As in Kevin Whitt, the attorney?"

I nodded.

"You do realize that Kevin Whitt is one of the top criminal attorneys in the state? And he has a tough reputation."

"Yes. I've been warned," I said.

"He's considered good people, Kate. He has connections in every branch of our government. If you go after his son..."

"He was out late that night, Chief, and he doesn't have an alibi. Just some cockamamie story that he was deer hunting, illegally. Spotlighting, he called it."

Johnston stared at me. "So you intend to bring him in?"

"Not right now, no," I replied. "I'm not sure he has it in him. Lindsey Waller was his ex-girlfriend, and she dumped him. Jealousy is a strong motive, but we're still digging. If I bring him in now, Kevin Whitt will be all over it and, as you say, it would get messy."

I paused for a second, then continued, "I don't think he's smart enough, Chief. This killer's good. So far, he's not made a single mistake. Mike's team has not found a single piece of evidence at either scene, aside from the two bullets. Though Lindsey Waller thinks she saw him in the distance. She thinks it was a man, but he was too far away and it was too dark."

"I still think you need to go after Rogan, *hard*," he said after a few moments of thought. "We need to be seen to be doing something, and Rogan fits the bill."

I got it. It was ass covering time. Never mind the damage it could do to the innocent. He did have a point, though. No matter how I felt personally about

Rogan, I couldn't prove anything, one way or the other. Not yet.

"I also think you should stay away from Ben Whitt," Johnston said, frowning as he stared at me. "For your own good. And because I doubt he had any part in it. How old is he? Eighteen? Nineteen? Boys his age... He probably *was* out spotlighting."

What bothered me about what he was saying was that I thought he was saying it for the wrong reasons. He didn't want the PD to become embroiled in a fight with the kid's father.

Geez, I hate these political games. I mean, so what if Kevin Whitt came after us? If his son was the killer, he needed to be taken off the streets, and I was going to do it.

But, sitting there in front of Johnston's desk, all I could do was nod and keep my mouth shut. Luckily, though, the chief wasn't done, and he continued on with his monologue as if I wasn't in the room.

"We're going to get crucified for this," he said, fingering his chin. "The city council is already talking about putting out a warning for teens to stay indoors after dark. There's even talk of a curfew. If we're not careful, the whole nation is going to think that Chattanooga is being plagued by a serial killer, and I do not want the FBI crawling all over us, and neither do you."

"Chief," I said after a moment of careful consideration, "I understand where you're coming from, but maybe an official warning wouldn't be a bad thing. If this killer is focused on teens, let's not make it easy for him."

Johnston locked eyes with me. I didn't envy him his

position. He had to play the middleman and, sitting across from him, I could see the man who had come up through the ranks was still there, just beneath the surface, conflicted, trying to do what he thought was best for both the department and his detectives.

"And if we ask the press to do that," he said, "it will make it look as if we're incapable of doing our job: to protect and serve. No. We're not going there; not yet. All right, Kate. That will be all, for now. Keep me posted. I want to know the minute anything breaks... And remember what I said. Watch out for Kevin Whitt."

"I will," I said and stood up. So did Samson, who'd been sitting quietly by my side the whole time.

I stopped half way out the door, turned again and said, "Thanks, Chief."

Johnston was under a lot of pressure, and I was feeling it, too. Not because of the press, the mayor, the city council, or even the chief, but because I didn't want anyone else to die.

27

Wednesday afternoon, 2:00 p.m.

I SPENT THE REST OF THE MORNING CATCHING UP ON the growing pile of paperwork on my desk, but my heart and my head weren't in it. When were they ever? I also called a meeting for two o'clock that afternoon.

Dani and Cooper were the last to arrive in the conference room, and by the look on their faces, they hadn't had a good morning.

Hawk, in the middle of wolfing down a burger, stopped in mid-chew and stared at them.

"What's up with you two?" I asked as they sat down at the table.

Dani smiled tentatively, but it was more of a grimace than a smile. "Um... we couldn't find Gabe Corewall."

There was a moment of silence while we all contemplated the news.

"What do you mean, couldn't find him?" Corbin asked, looking from Dani to Cooper and back again.

"We stopped by his house twice and he wasn't there," Cooper said. "And we checked at his workplace, too. He didn't come in this morning. We checked with some of his friends. They didn't know where he is either." He shrugged.

I leaned back in my chair and stared at Cooper, not really seeing him, my mind in a whirl. I had a really bad feeling about it, and I remembered the chief's insistence that Nathaniel Rogan was tied up in it somehow, and if Corewall had gone missing, it sure as hell didn't look good for him.

"So not only are we unable to verify Rogan's alibi," I said, "we can't find the guy he was supposed to be with that night. That's just too much of a coincidence."

Dani hesitated for a second, then said, "Yeah. It looks that way."

"Did you talk to his boss?" I asked.

She shook her head. "No. He's off today, it being Wednesday. He'll be in tomorrow."

A stream of scenarios went flying through my head, each discarded as crazy but also possible; the worst of which was...

Had Gabe really been with Nathaniel that night? Had he seen something he shouldn't have? And had Rogan gotten rid of him?

"We're going to stop by his house again this afternoon," Cooper said. "But we wanted to check in with you first. If he's not there, I was thinking we could stop by Rogan's and see if he knows where he is. If not, we could ask him to try and get hold of him. Like for his own benefit, you know?"

"Good idea," I said. "This is not looking good for him. If anything's happened to Corewall, he'll be moving to the top of the list. Anne, Hawk, what did you learn from Jasmine and Brad Herbert?"

"They both have solid alibis," Anne said. "They're clean. You can eliminate them."

I looked at Hawk. He nodded.

"Well, that's something, I suppose," I said, thinking hard.

It was then that Jack spoke up. He'd been looking over the case file again, "I think I know someone who can help," he said.

"And who would that be?" I asked.

He made a face, then said, "It may be nothing..."

I could tell by the look on his face that he didn't want to tell me, which meant it probably involved one of his computer "specialist" acquaintances, so I nodded and gave him the benefit of the doubt and said, "Whatever it is, Jack, be careful what you say and how much. Be discreet."

"You got it, boss," he said happily, then got to his feet, gathered up his paperwork and left.

"I need something to eat," I said. "Y'all know what to do, right?" I looked at them. They all nodded, then upped and followed Jack out into the situation room.

I did the same, only I was headed to Smokey's BBQ

for something to fill the void in my gut, though I had a feeling it wasn't food that I needed to fill it.

Be that as it may, I was hungry, and the smokey smell wafting in through the open window of my SUV as I sat in the line at the drive-thru was intoxicating. I'd already placed my order and was next in line to the window with my foot on the brake, staring blankly ahead when, in my peripheral vision, I spotted a familiar face: Cindy Davis, the mother of our first victim, Caroline Davis. She was walking through the parking lot of the strip mall next door, carrying what looked like a prescription bag.

I yanked down on the steering wheel, ignoring the shout of the employee at the drive-thru window, and swung the car out of the drive-thru line and into the strip mall parking lot. I applied the brake, opened the door, jumped out and shouted, "Hey! Mrs. Davis!"

28

Wednesday afternoon, 2:45 p.m.

For some reason, Cindy Davis wasn't pleased to
see me.

"What is it?" she asked, obviously annoyed. "D'you
have an update for me? If not, I'm in a hurry and can't
talk right now."

"It's not that," I said, catching up with her as she
continued walking slowly toward her Kia, shoulders back,
back straight and stiff, the prescription bag clenched
tightly in her fist.

"Mrs. Davis, please," I said, putting a hand on her
arm. "I just need a moment. I won't keep you long. I
promise. I think you might be able to help."

Actually, I didn't. In fact, I didn't know why I
stopped her at all. It was just one of those feelings I get
from time to time. Anyway, it caught her attention. She

paused next to her car, turned and looked at me as if she was assessing me.

Her eyes were rimmed with red, and I immediately felt sorry for her. She looked tired, and I figured she probably hadn't been sleeping much. I resisted the urge to glance at the paper bag in her hand, wondering who the prescription was for and what it was for.

Without a doubt, Sarah, Mr. Davis, and the entire family would be grieving deeply, especially Sarah, who would, no doubt, still be feeling guilty.

"Very well," she said. "How can I help?"

"Does the name Nathaniel Rogan mean anything to you, Mrs. Davis? Did Caroline ever mention him?"

She frowned, then said, "No. I don't know anyone by that name, and Caroline never mentioned the name either. Why? Is he a suspect?"

I tried to hide my disappointment, and I couldn't help but wonder if I'd made a mistake revealing the name to her. All she had to do was go home and Google the name, and she'd find the old news articles about Rogan's arrest and the debacle at the state park. And when she did, I had no doubt she'd talk about it and, like everyone else, including the chief, want to know why we hadn't just arrested him. I had a feeling my case was about to turn into a nightmare.

"No," I said. "Not at all. He's a neighbor who lives nearby, and we're just trying to find out if Caroline or Jared knew anyone in the area," I explained, hoping to alleviate her suspicions. It wasn't an outright lie, but it wasn't the full truth, either. Would it be enough to throw her off the ex-con's trail? I hoped so, and quickly changed the subject.

"How about Ben Whitt or Luke Webber?" I asked. "Did she know either of them?"

"Ben Whitt? Yes, of course, Caroline knew Ben," she replied, perking up a little. "Oh no! You don't think... You can't think that Ben Whitt is involved, do you?"

Now she had me curious. It had just been a shot in the dark, the first name that'd popped into my head. They were almost the same age, and I figured it was likely they'd attended the same high school.

I ignored her question and said, "How did they know each other? Were they at school together?"

Davis nodded and said, "Yes. They were at high school together and dated for a while."

What? I nearly choked in surprise. "They dated?" I asked, keeping my expression blank.

"Yes, during Caroline's freshman and sophomore years. They broke up right before summer. Caroline ended it, and Ben started seeing someone else."

Yes, I thought. *Lindsey Waller.*

"Did they get along well?" I asked. "When they were dating?"

"Oh, yes," she replied, frowning. "Of course. They were just kids at the time. They spent most of their time hanging out at our house or at the Whitts'. Ben was always very polite. He's a nice boy."

Yeah, I could see that. Although I'd experienced Ben's teenage attitude, arrogance and sarcasm, I could imagine how his family would have raised their boy with good manners.

"So Caroline never had any issues with him, Ben?" I asked. "It was an amicable breakup, just a normal teenage thing?"

And there it was; she hesitated, then said, "No. Not exactly... amicable."

"What does that mean, Mrs. Davis?" She looked at me, obviously reluctant to talk about the boy.

"It's all right," I said. "You can tell me what happened."

"But you can't think Ben..." She laughed breathily. I could tell she was nervous. I said nothing. Instead, I waited for her to continue.

"It wasn't an amicable breakup," she said finally. "It was when Caroline was still confiding in me. You know, coming to me to talk about her life, her friends, her relationships. But then all that stopped." She grimaced, and I could read between the lines. It would have been when she'd gotten involved with Jared Moore that those secret-spilling conversations between mother and daughter had stopped.

"Why did Caroline break up with Ben?" I asked.

"She didn't really tell me. I was disappointed, but she was very sure. I mean, Ben Whitt. His family is very well off, you know. His father is a prominent attorney, and his mother was a member of the PTA with me."

"So you wanted her to try and work it out with him?" I said.

She glanced away. She had that guilty look of a

mother who tried to push her children into something she thought was right for them, even if it wasn't what they wanted.

"I just told her to be sure," she replied.

"What did you think of him?" I asked.

"Before the breakup, I liked him. After, well, I saw them arguing once, and the look on his face..." She trailed off.

"So," I said, "When Caroline decided to break up with him, how did he take it?"

She sighed. "Not well, I think, which was to be expected. He really loved Caroline; at least he said he did. You know, the way teenagers do, but I think it was probably more of an infatuation. I do remember that Caroline was exhausted the day they broke up, and for days after, he texted her a lot. He even called Sarah a couple of times."

"Would I be right in saying that it didn't quite end there?" I asked.

She nodded. "About three weeks after the breakup, Ben showed up at the house. It was really late, past eleven. I remember because the dog woke us up barking. Ben was outside yelling up at Caroline's window. She didn't want to go down and open the front door. My husband had to go down and make him leave, but even then..." She glanced sideways at me. "He had to threaten to call the police, and then Ben left, finally. He didn't show up at the house again like that, but for a while I'd see his truck parked down the street."

"You're sure it was him?" I asked, frowning, thinking

that my instincts had been right about Ben Whitt after all. There was something off about that kid.

"Oh, yes. It was him all right. That red pickup truck is unmistakable. It looks ridiculous all raised up like that, and with all the floodlights."

She was right. That pickup was hard to miss.

"So Ben kept showing up after the breakup," I said. "Did Caroline ever say if she felt threatened, or unsafe?"

"No. I asked her, but she kept insisting that everything was fine and that he'd get over it. I think by then she'd met Jared, and maybe that's when Ben found someone else to focus on because I didn't see him around after that. But for a few weeks there, I was uncomfortable with him lingering around the way he did."

"And you never reported it to the police?"

She shook her head. "No. I don't know if you know, but Ben's father is a lawyer, and I didn't want there to be any bad blood between us. I didn't want..." She trailed off.

I knew exactly what she didn't want. She didn't want to get sued, and I didn't blame her.

"So after the breakup and the summer, everything was okay between Caroline and Ben Whitt?"

Cindy shrugged. "Yeah. I mean, they didn't interact much. Caroline did her own thing. And Ben started seeing some trashy girl. Lindsey something, I think her name was."

Trashy. That was a bit harsh.

She obviously didn't know that Lindsey Waller was another victim. Despite Lindsey being legally an adult, the press, per our request, had kept her name out of their reports. For how much longer, though, I didn't know. But I wasn't hopeful that knowing Lindsey was a victim would inspire compassion in Mrs. Davis. No. She seemed the kind of woman who would only be bitter that Lindsey had lived while Caroline had died.

"Well," I said. "I've taken up enough of your time, Mrs. Davis. Thank you. You've been very helpful."

I turned away, gave her a quick wave and headed back to my car, where Samson had his nose on the window.

Me? I was thinking there was a lot more to Ben Whitt than any of us had initially thought. The boy had a nasty streak in him, and he obviously didn't like it when the girl broke up with him.

Maybe it was time to bite the bullet and bring him in. Put a little pressure on him. See if he cracked, or not.

"Okay, Sammy," I said, climbing in behind the wheel. "Let's go get something to eat."

I heard his jaws snap behind me, and I smiled, and not just because of that. No. I had something new to hang my hat on: Ben Whitt.

29

Wednesday afternoon, 4 p.m.

NO SOONER HAD I SAT BACK DOWN AT MY DESK THAN Corbin popped his head in, holding up a folder.

"I have Willis' report," he said. "Want a run-down?"

"Sure," I said, gesturing to the chair in front of my desk.

He sat down, made himself comfortable and dug right in.

"The two cases are definitely connected. Aside from the weapon being the same type, ballistics matched the two bullets. They came from the same gun. Mike also found—get this—tire tracks."

"Dual rear-wheel drive?" I guessed.

Corbin nodded.

"Were they able to make casts?" I asked.

"Yup."

"Well, that's good. Now we have something to run by Johnston. I'll give him the good news later."

Corbin gave me a small smile. I wasn't ready to tell the chief about Ben Whitt yet. I didn't want him going off on me again, not until I was reasonably sure.

Anyway, the news was good. Now we had to make sure there wasn't a third attack.

"So," I said. "I ran into Cindy Davis earlier this afternoon, and I learned something interesting."

"Caroline's mom, you mean?" he asked. "And she was okay talking to you?"

"Well, she wasn't happy to see me. But we had an interesting conversation."

I quickly filled him in, highlighting the main points. When I'd finished, he just sat there staring at me. He actually looked a little stunned, which was unusual because nothing ever fazed Corbin.

"That's..."

"Yes," I replied emphatically. "It's incredible, but here's the problem. The chief told me to stay away from the Whitts. Ben Whitt specifically."

Corbin nodded. We both knew what that meant if we decided to move forward.

"I get you," he said. "But we can't just ignore it. It can't be just a coincidence, can it? I mean, come on. Even he would agree we have to follow it through, right?"

I nodded thoughtfully. "We need to talk to Ben," I said. "He's an adult, so we can pick him up and talk to him without his parents in attendance."

"That's true, but as soon as he asks for a lawyer..."

"Kevin Whitt will show up," I said and heaved a sigh.

"And, him being the son of a lawyer," Corbin continued, "he'll know to do that, and quickly."

I sat back in my chair and put my hands behind my neck.

"Maybe we can catch him off balance," I said. "Maybe we're wrong. If he has nothing to hide, he should talk to us."

"I mean, we can try," Corbin said, but he didn't sound convinced. I wasn't either. I knew we were walking a very thin line, and I wouldn't have been surprised if, as soon as Johnston heard we had Ben Whitt in an interview room, he showed up and shut us down.

My problem was that I was now thinking of Ben Whitt as a viable suspect, but I was still in no position to pursue him. If I did, his father would close us down before we could even get started; Chief Johnston, too.

There was a knock on the door. It opened, and Robar stepped in.

"Captain. Corbin," she said, "I just wanted to let you know that Hawk and I might have the tail end of a lead."

I waved her in. Corbin scooted his chair over to make room for her.

"Talk to me," I said. "What've you got?" I was beginning to feel that the day was shaping up to be too good to be true.

"Well," she began, "during our conversation with Brad Herbert and Jasmine Hall, some familiar names came up."

"Brad and Jasmine both have alibis for the shooting

last night, right?" They'd already said as much, but I hadn't had time to go through their report.

"Yes," she replied. "Solid, too. They were at a bar with several friends." Anne caught Corbin's look and added, "Yes, Corbin. We checked with their friends, too. Four different people confirmed that the pair was there until almost one a.m. Anyway, we threw out some names to see if we could get a reaction, since Jasmine apparently knew Caroline. And Jasmine mentioned that she did, in fact, know Nathaniel Rogan."

I shook my head and narrowed my eyes to the point where I could barely see out of them.

"You're kidding me," I snapped. If true, it complicated things more than I cared to contemplate. Two minutes ago, I was *sure* Ben Whitt was good for it. Now Nathaniel Rogan was back in the mix.

Anne had said that Jasmine also knew Daniel Thomas, one of our victims. Apparently, they went to school together. She connected Dan and Rogan. She said they both worked at the same lumber yard. Lyon & Holmes, the same place where Chase Richards worked. One of the first places I'd stopped on this wild goose chase. It was all coming full circle, in some weird kind of way.

"Did you confirm it?" I asked, wondering how in the hell we'd overlooked Rogan's workplace.

"Yes. Hawk made the call earlier to the manager. Rogan was let go about a month ago. Apparently, the owners found out about his prison record and wanted him out of there, so the manager let him go with some sorry excuse."

"What was the excuse?"

"That Rogan's PO appointments were taking precedence over his job. As they should. Hawk and I checked in with Rogan again just to confirm it, and he insisted it was all a bunch of BS, too. I'm not arguing with him on that. His PO was willing to move the appointments to whenever, so Rogan could keep his job, but the lumber yard let him go anyway."

"So how does Daniel Thomas tie into all this, again?"

"Dan Thomas was planning on going to college for accounting. He was working part-time at the lumber yard, two days a week for a pretty measly hourly rate. That's how he met Rogan."

"And Rogan told you all this?" Corbin asked.

"Yes. He says they met at the lumber yard and that they used to coon hunt a lot, but Daniel was too busy lately, so Rogan hadn't seen him in a while. That's when he started coon hunting with Gabe Corewall."

We stared at each other in silence for a moment. I was trying to assimilate this new information. It totally reshaped what I was thinking. I'd been ready to eliminate him as a suspect, but now... Now he was directly tied to one of the victims.

"Look," I said. "We asked Lisa Thomas if she knew anyone who might have had a problem with Daniel. She must have known about Rogan. It was all over the news for weeks. And Daniel would have told her about him. He must have, if he was going coon hunting with him, right? But she didn't point the finger at Rogan. Why didn't she mention him?"

"And she doesn't exactly approve of ex-cons, does she?" Corbin added, giving me a knowing look. He was referring to Daniel's dad.

"D'you think she was aware of the friendship but didn't see a problem with it?" Anne asked.

"Maybe," I replied. "It seems highly unlikely that she didn't know about him."

Oh, what a tangled web we weave, I thought, quoting Sir Walter Scott to myself.

30

Wednesday evening, 5:00 p.m.

"You sure you two are up for this?" I asked Robar and Hawk as we stood together in the entrance to the police department, uniformed officers coming and going. Corbin had taken Samson out front for a quick break. "I can always get Dani and Cooper on it if you want to get some rest." They, too, had been on their feet almost constantly for the last four days.

Hawk shook his head and crossed his beefy arms. "We've got it, Captain. I'd like to see this one through to the end, and I'm sure Anne feels the same way."

Anne nodded, her steel-gray hair glinting in the late afternoon light. I felt bad sending them back out when they both had families at home, families that would soon be sitting down for dinner. Me? I had my own hoops to jump through; another load of boxes to drop off at my new house. I only had two weeks left on my apartment lease, so I had to move everything out by then, even if it was slow-going.

But Anne and Hawk had pulled this particular thread and wanted to follow up with Lisa Thomas themselves. They were about to go and find out what she knew about Daniel and Nathaniel Rogan.

I was dying of curiosity, too, though still distracted by Ben Whitt. There were just too many bad vibes surrounding that kid.

"All right," I said, "but do the paperwork at home, and don't come back here unless you absolutely have to, okay? Text me updates."

The pair headed out. Corbin returned with Samson.

"What do you think?" I said, leaning on the side of the building. It was a nice evening, and good to get a breath of fresh air to offload the crushing weight of all the new complications.

"I don't know *what* to think," he admitted. "Just when we set our sights on one suspect..."

"Right? I know Johnston wants us to focus on Rogan, but I'm thinking we should bring in Ben Whitt."

Samson tugged at his leash, pulling Corbin over to the side. "You're thinking Rogan isn't good for it?"

I already knew by the look on Corbin's face that he wasn't convinced, either. It was good to know we were on the same page. "No. It doesn't fit. It's such a specific MO."

"You're right," Corbin said, "it doesn't fit. Rogan didn't exactly try to hide when he stabbed that guy in Booker T. Washington Park, did he?"

"There's something going on here that I just can't nail down," I said, watching traffic go by as the 9-to-5ers returned home for the night. "There's something going on here, and I have no idea what it is. And now we know that all the victims are tied together. So why? That's the big question. Why is someone killing these kids? What's the motive?"

I looked at Corbin. He shrugged, obviously as frustrated as I was.

"I think we need to bring Whitt in," I continued. "Something is off with that kid, and we need to find out what it is. His alibi's weak, and I don't like what Cindy Davis had to say."

"I get it," he said. "I've been doing a little digging. Whitt works at a horse ranch."

"Oh, yes? What ranch?"

"Silver Waters," he replied.

I hadn't heard of it. "Let's do it," I said. "Where is it?"

"It's out in the county, about a twenty-minute ride. You want to take a cruiser, or keep it under cover?"

We opted for my unmarked SUV. I didn't want Ben getting spooked and disappearing to call his dad before we had a chance to speak with him. Samson hopped into the back as Corbin settled into the passenger seat.

Inwardly, I shook my head. I was about to step over the line. I was going after a suspect I'd been specifically told to stay away from and, whether or not Ben Whitt was our killer, Chief Johnston wouldn't be happy.

It was almost five-thirty when we arrived at Silver Waters. It was now early December and the place looked pretty bleak.

The house itself was a nice, white two-story affair surrounded by nicely manicured Bermuda grass lawns. Two barns, one on either side of the house, were set at an angle, forming a sort of stiff-sided crescent. In front of the barn to the right was a black F-350 with dual rear wheels. It hadn't been at the Whitts' house the day we went to speak to Ben.

I looked at Corbin. He nodded. He'd spotted it too.

"See anyone?" I asked.

Corbin shook his head, his hand on the door handle.

I got out of the truck and looked around. There were several horses and a donkey in a field next to a small stand of elm trees. It was quiet, save for the odd whicker from the horses.

Corbin joined me, and after considering my options, I let Samson out on his leash. I didn't need him chasing after the horses.

"Let's try there," Corbin said, looking at the barn where the F-350 was parked.

I nodded, and together we walked toward the barn.

We were just feet away when Ben Whitt stepped out carrying a bucket full of what I figured must have been food for the horses. He was also wearing a serious pair of headphones.

He stopped dead when he saw us, obviously startled. Then, his expression turned grim. He put down the bucket and removed the headphones. He was wearing a dark blue roll-neck sweater, blue jeans and heavy, black work boots.

"What do you want?" he asked harshly.

"Hello again, Ben. We just want to talk," I replied.

Corbin gave him a nod. Samson sat, his tail curving around my right heel, his gaze fixed on Whitt.

He glared at Corbin, his eyes narrowed, his forehead furrowed, and, for just a moment, I saw something in him, something that had probably scared Cindy Davis. There was an intensity about him.

"I don't have anything to talk to you about."

"Well, that's too bad," I said, "because we have plenty to talk about."

"Well, you can't," he snapped. "Can't you see I'm working? I have to feed the horses. So why don't you go harass someone else."

I didn't take kindly to the word "harass." It had legal implications, and I could just imagine his father taking it up with the chief.

"Mr. Whitt," Corbin said, his voice quiet, calm, "I think it would be best if you joined us at the police department. You can drive yourself. But we are going to talk."

"Did you not hear what I just said?" he spat out, his eyes flashing with anger.

"Oh, we heard you," I said. "You have two choices. You can either drive yourself down to the station, or I can call for backup and have your ass hauled in. Which is it to be?"

He opened his mouth to speak, and I fully expected

him to invoke his father, but then Samson stood up and growled, and Whitt's eyes flicked to the shepherd and his mouth clamped shut. He swallowed hard and then did the last thing I expected. He agreed.

"All right. I'll follow you down there. But I'm not staying long, and I have to finish up here first. It won't take but a few minutes, okay?"

I nodded. He grabbed the bucket—of what I learned later was oats—and headed to the trough just inside the gated field where the half-dozen horses were waiting.

31

Wednesday evening, 6:45 p.m.

BACK AT THE DEPARTMENT, CORBIN SETTLED BEN Whitt down in the interrogation room and then joined me next door, where we watched him on the monitor.

He was obviously uncomfortable, constantly pulling at the neck of his sweater, glancing around, looking at the camera, kicking his legs out and then bringing them back in again, fidgeting on his seat.

"He's kind of nervous, right?" Corbin asked as we stood together in front of the monitor.

"Oh, yeah," I replied. "Too bad we couldn't bring the chief in to see this without him busting a vein. He'll pitch a fit when he finds out we've brought him in."

But, in truth, it was only a matter of time until Chief Johnston found out that we had Ben Whitt in an interrogation room. And it was also only a matter of time until Ben Whitt got smart and called his dad.

"Do you want first dibs?" I asked.

Corbin tried to mask a grin as he nodded, then stepped out into the corridor.

"Hey, Ben," he said as he stepped into the interrogation room. "You okay? Can I get you something to drink, a Coke, water?"

Whitt shook his head, stretched out his legs, folded his arms across his chest and stared at Corbin as he sat down opposite him.

"Thank you again for coming in," Corbin began. "I just have a few questions for you. It won't take long if you're straight with me. Understand?"

Whitt continued to stare at him, his mouth working as if he had a chaw of dip in his lip, but after a couple of seconds, he nodded.

"When we spoke the other day, you told us you'd been out spotlighting. Would you like to elaborate?"

Whitt drew in his legs but remained slouched on the chair, a half-smirk on his lips.

He shook his head, thought about it for a second or two —Corbin had a lot more patience with him than I would have had—then he shrugged and said, "Sorry. It is what it is. I was out, by myself. You'll just have to take my word for it."

"That's not much of an alibi, is it, Ben?"

Again, Whitt shrugged but said nothing.

"All right," Corbin said. "Let's move on. Your name came up earlier today."

Whitt's eyes locked onto Corbin's. "Oh, yeah? How come?"

"Captain Gazzara happened to be talking to Mrs. Davis. Caroline Davis' mother. You didn't tell us that you and Caroline dated when you were in high school."

Whitt smirked, shifted his backside on his seat and said, "So?"

"So why didn't you tell us?" Corbin snapped.

Whitt flinched, then recovered and said, "You didn't ask, did you?"

"True," Corbin said. "But you knew we were investigating Caroline's murder, and you didn't think you should mention that you were, or had been, involved with her? That's kind of strange, don't you think?"

He shrugged. "No. Not really. It was a while ago. More than a year ago now, I think."

I shook my head at that. I was willing to bet that he knew exactly, probably down to the day and time, how long it had been since they'd split up.

I watched as Corbin settled back in his chair, folded his arms, smiled at him and said, "Here's the thing, Ben. We know you and Caroline dated for what, almost two years? We also know that it didn't end well, did it? You couldn't let go, could you? You stalked the girl. That doesn't look good. Does it, Ben?"

He frowned, seemed less confident, but it didn't last. He just shook his head and smirked. "So I was upset, so what? We'd been together a long time. You'd be upset, too. But no. I wouldn't say it 'didn't end well.'"

"That's not what her mother told Captain Gazzara; just the opposite, in fact," Corbin replied.

Whitt's lip twitched as if he was about to say something, but Corbin continued on. "In fact, she said her husband had to warn you off. Didn't he threaten to call the police when you—"

"That's not how it happened," Whitt snapped and, for a moment, I thought he was going to lose his temper, but then he seemed to get hold of himself. "That's not what happened," he said. "I went over to talk to Caroline—"

"Didn't you think it was a little late at night for that?"

"*No*," he insisted. "No. Caroline's always up late. She's a night owl. I knew she'd be up, and I just wanted to talk to her."

Something about what he'd said was digging at me like a splinter.

Or rather, how he'd said it.

He used the present tense. *Caroline's* always up late. It wasn't much. Nothing at all, really, but it caught my attention. He was still thinking of her in the present tense, meaning it wasn't yet lodged in his brain that she was deceased. And the only conclusion I could draw from that was that he hadn't killed her.

Once again, Corbin let the silence stretch on before asking, "Don't you think you were a little intense, a little over the top, maybe? After all, according to Mrs. Davis, Caroline had made it pretty clear it was over and that she wanted nothing more to do with you."

Whitt stared at him, obviously angry at the way the interview was going, but then, once again, he seemed to calm down. "Okay. So maybe I was. I was... upset. I really liked her. I loved her. If you're thinking I killed her, you're wrong. I wouldn't... I couldn't."

It seemed to me that, like most teens, Ben only thought he knew what love was. I was just about ready to pull the plug on the interview when Corbin switched directions.

"How about Lindsey Waller?" he asked. "Was your breakup with her a bad one, too?"

Whitt was visibly taken aback by the question. His eyes narrowed and he sat up straight, staring at Corbin through his messy bangs. "What? No. No!"

"So," Corbin said quietly. "What happened? Why did you two break up?"

"It wasn't nothing like you're thinking," he said. "Lindsey was just too much, you know? She always insisted on doing what she wanted to do, and I wasn't into being dragged around like that, so we ended it."

Corbin leaned forward to say something when Ben's eyes narrowed.

"Okay. That's enough," Ben said. "I can see where you're going with this. I think I need a lawyer. Call my dad, please."

Corbin pursed his lips, nodded, and he stood up. As soon as the interrogation room door closed behind him, I heaved a deep sigh and shook my head.

"Johnston's not going to like this, Corbin," I said as he stepped into the observation room."

Corbin looked surprised. "You think so? I don't—"

I shook my head. "You didn't catch it, did you? He referred to Caroline in the present tense. You do realize what that means, right? Deep down, he's not yet fully accepted that she's dead. I don't think he did it."

Corbin stared at me as he came to grips with what I was saying.

"Darn," he said, shaking his head. "Okay. Well, should we even bother keeping him here? We may as well just let him go."

"I think that's probably the best idea. He isn't our guy."

"What about that truck?" he said. "It fits the profile."

"We'd need a warrant to check the tires," I replied. "Come on."

Ben was sitting upright, his forearms on the table, hands clasped together.

"Ben," I began. "You don't need a lawyer. You're not under arrest. We're going to let you go. You've been very cooperative and helpful. Thank you. But if you don't mind, I do have one more question for you before you go, okay?"

He wasn't happy, but he nodded and seemed to relax.

"That truck you're driving. Is it yours? I only ask because when we first met you, you were driving a red pickup, and we also saw it at your house."

He glared at me, then at Corbin, then back at me again. "I drive whatever I want," he snapped. "Whenever I want. Can I go now?"

"It's not yours, then?" I said.

"And I said, can I go now?"

I shook my head, then said, "Show him out, Sergeant."

32

IT WAS ALMOST NINE O'CLOCK. SAMSON AND I WERE still in my office. I was trying to catch up on some paperwork, but my heart wasn't in it. It had been just after six when we'd turned Ben Whitt loose, and I was still wondering about the repercussions yet to come.

And so I sat there at my desk, staring unseeing at the pile of files, mulling it over, trying to figure out what my next step was going to be. And, to boot, I was probably going to find myself in trouble in the morning.

I hadn't been able to get Chief Johnston the answers he wanted. Anne and Hawk hadn't been able to find Gabe Corewall; nope, Rogan's coon-hunting "friend" seemed to have disappeared; gone off the map.

I tapped the pile of folders, checked the time, then my phone to see if Cooper had gotten my text about him and Dani checking in with Rogan first thing the following morning. He had. Then, after a last glance at the stack of folders, I clicked my tongue and Samson jumped up from his bed.

I took the long way home that night. I drove by my new —to me—house, thinking about the stacks of cardboard boxes in the living room, and those still back in my apartment. The house was dark and, set back from the road as it was, difficult to see. Even so, it was hard to imagine it was mine. It still didn't seem real that I was now a homeowner, and I still didn't quite know how I felt about it; it was all kind of... surreal.

As we drove by, I scanned my soon-to-be next-door neighbor's house. Amber light spilled from the windows out into the yard, and I could see a shadowy figure moving around inside. I imagined laughter, the feeling of being surrounded by family and friends... something I'd never really known... and I suddenly felt lonely, also something I hadn't felt in quite a while. I'd never before had time for it.

I pulled into my apartment parking space feeling... I don't know, out of sorts, as they say.

Samson must have felt my mood because he whined as I opened the rear door to let him out. I figured he must be as done in as I was with the working day.

I warmed up the last two slices of two-day-old pizza, poured Sam some kibbles and sprinkled some grated cheese over it, and we ate. Not the most satisfying dinner I'd ever eaten, but it filled the gap, and I felt a little better. Still consumed by the case, but better.

For about half an hour, I meandered around the

apartment. I picked up a book and then put it down again. I turned on the TV, then turned it off again. I stared out of the window, across the open space to East Brainerd Road and beyond, then I turned to Samson and said, "Hey!"

He perked up and tilted his head.

"You want to go for a run?"

He stood up and loped to the door.

I threw on a pair of sneakers and clipped on Samson's leash.

It was late for a run, but I needed it. I was mentally exhausted, but it wasn't the kind of exhaustion that would put me to sleep. In fact, I was totally frazzled. I had that awful feeling that my brain was fried, and I was unable to make sense of anything. I needed to clear my head, burn off some energy.

Out on the street, it was raining. Not hard, just a fine mist. Securing my ponytail with a hair tie, I threw the hood up over my head and smiled as Samson shook off the first layer of dew-like rain. His heavy coat of fur was like a thatched cottage; the rain just ran off it.

We started out at a light jog for maybe a half mile, then moved it up a little into an easy, long-legged stride. With the drizzle running down my face, I found it exhilarating as we ran on and on.

Samson seemed to be enjoying the run as much as I was as we followed our five-mile route, a shorter run than usual, but I didn't want to be out too late that night. Tomorrow, as Scarlett said, was another day, a day for paperwork and Chief Johnston, and I wasn't looking forward to it.

Anne and Hawk had the day off. Jack North was helping out another team with some tech issue I didn't completely understand, but then, I never did.

Tracy Ramirez was due back from her vacation that morning, and I'd spend some time catching her up on the case. Perfect time to do it, too, because I needed a fresh set of eyes, and Tracy's were pretty damn sharp.

And, of course, Cooper and Dani would be visiting our enigmatic friend, Nate Rogan, who, I hoped, would tell us where to find the elusive Gabe Corewall. I really didn't feel good about that guy going missing.

Five miles and some forty-five minutes later, we'd circled back to the apartment feeling somewhat better. At least I was. Samson slurped down a couple of pints of water and then trotted right over to his bed, flopped down and heaved a huge sigh.

I, on the other hand, felt re-energized. Probably not a good thing since it was close to ten o'clock and I needed to get to sleep.

I showered, dried my hair, and stood before the mirror brushing my teeth, staring myself down and wondering where the hell the youngster that once stared back at me had gone.

It was almost eleven when I finally climbed into bed that night, and I hadn't been under the covers for more than a few seconds when Samson slipped silently into the room, jumped up onto the bed, laid his head down on the pillow next to mine and sighed.

"I know," I said, turning toward him, propped up on one elbow. "It's a tough one, Sammy." That was putting it lightly. "You got any ideas, boy?"

He sighed again, rolling a big brown eye.

"Ben Whitt is off the list, unless something new comes up, of course. He has no alibi, but there's not much we can do about that. It doesn't mean he's a killer, does it?"

Samson kicked out his back legs.

"Then there's Rogan. Don't you think it's strange how everything keeps coming back to him? Chase Richards and Daniel Thomas both working at the same lumber yard where he was fired, and the only person who can confirm his alibi is missing."

Samson sighed again, wriggled, then closed his eyes.

"But see, it feels like it's too easy and..." I murmured, finally beginning to fall asleep, "we still can't prove anything, can we?"

My last, desperate thought as I started to drift off was, *We can't go jumping to conclusions. The chief might be convinced that he's an ex-con on the rampage, but it makes no sense. The pieces just don't fit.*

33

Thursday morning, 10:00 a.m.

"How's Ramirez doing?" Corbin asked as he slid into the passenger seat of my unmarked SUV.

Samson, happy to see him, gave his ear a wet willy with his nose, making him shudder.

"She's good," I replied, smiling as I pulled out of the lot. "She was quiet most of the time I was briefing her. I think the vacation did her good. They went to Mexico, you know, Cabo San Lucas."

"What did she say?" he asked as I turned left onto Amnicola. "Anything? A new perspective? What?"

"No. Not really, though she does agree that Rogan doesn't fit the MO."

"Oh," Corbin muttered, "good thing we're heading to his place, then."

Dani and Cooper had stopped by his place twice the

day before and earlier that morning, but they hadn't seen him. So where the hell was he? I decided to go see for myself, a selfish choice made mostly because I wanted to dodge the stack of paperwork on my desk, and the chief, at least for a little while.

I was in a bad mood, and so was the weather. The sky was overcast and dull; perfect.

Fifteen minutes later we were pulling into Rogan's drive, seeing that little cabin reveal itself all over again. Once more, I just couldn't get it through my head that an ex-con who had all that would be willing to toss it away for a few dead teens. Rogan was smarter than that.

This time, we got lucky. His truck was parked in the driveway.

"All right, then," Corbin said as he opened the car door and stepped out.

Samson leapt over onto the passenger seat and followed him out.

Before I could round the SUV, the sound of snarling and snapping broke out. I bolted around to the passenger side, where Corbin was shouting, "Off! Off! Off!"

That bruiser of a coonhound was going for Samson, coming in low and trying to go for his throat. Samson barked and snapped, his head and shoulders low to the ground, his huge teeth bared, and he wasn't smiling.

"Hey! Brutus! Come!"

Nate Rogan stepped out onto the front porch, and the coonhound immediately turned and trotted to him. The dog's head was hanging as if he knew he'd done something bad. It circled around behind Rogan and sat at his side, ears flattened.

Rogan slowly descended the steps, his hands at his side, and he didn't look happy to see us.

"Sorry about that, Captain," he said, glancing at my badge on my belt, then at Corbin with a nod and said, "Detective. Brutus is protective, which is a good thing around here."

I tried to give him the benefit of the doubt and replied, "Not the worst thing. No harm, no foul."

The two dogs hadn't gotten to actual fighting, so no harm had been done. But I wouldn't have given much for the coonhound's chances if it had. I had a feeling one-hundred-fifteen-pound Samson would have made short work of him. Still, his dog was just protecting his property, and I couldn't fault him for that.

Corbin, on the other hand, looked a little shaken as he returned Rogan's greeting.

"How can I help you?" the ex-con asked in a somewhat resigned tone. I tried to hide a smile. I think he must have gotten the clue that we were sticking around until the case was solved.

"We're still looking for your hunting pal, Gabe Corewall," I said, gesturing for Sammy to come, which he did and sat down quietly at my side, only occasionally glaring at the porch where the coonhound was sitting. "He seems to have gone missing, and without him, we can't confirm your alibi. Any idea where he might be?"

"Coon hunting," he said, looking back and forth at

Corbin and me. "If not that, I'm not sure where he could be. I haven't heard from him since Monday, and that's the damn truth. And it ain't unusual..."

"The problem is," Corbin said, "it puts us in a tight spot. If we can't confirm where you were that morning, we can't rule you out as a suspect."

The tendons in Rogan's jaw flexed. And then he did something I hadn't expected.

"Would you two like to sit down? I was just putting on another pot of coffee."

Corbin and I shared a quick glance. I nodded, and we followed him up to the cabin. Samson and Brutus, the coonhound, circled each other several times, tails wagging low, as the three of us waited until they made their peace, and then we went into the house.

It was small but well-kept. More than enough for one man and a couple of dogs. The front door opened into a combined living-kitchen-dining area, all with rustic-looking pine furniture.

CORBIN and I took a seat at the table, and as I looked around, to me, it didn't look like the home of a psycho killer. Everything was neat, tidy and in its place. It was a nice home. And it only made me more convinced that Rogan wasn't the guy we were looking for.

Rogan returned to the table with a classic coffee pot and three mugs. He poured one for each of us, then sat down, a grim look on his face.

"Look," he began, wrapping an overly large hand around his own mug, "I know how this looks, okay? I'm well aware of what everyone thinks of me. But I had nothing to do with these shootings. I don't own a gun. I use traps when I go hunting, and most of the time, I just go for the dogs."

"I get it," I said, "but until we can prove you aren't involved, we're sticking around. So tell me, does Gabe Corewall own a gun?"

Rogan frowned and said, "Well, yeah."

"Okay, so that's a problem right there," I said. "You admit you were out late, right around the time of the murders, with a guy who owns a gun and who is now MIA."

His face twisted up in annoyance. "I told you. I know how it looks, but I don't know where Gabe is—"

"Mr. Rogan, we're not accusing you of anything," Corbin cut in firmly. "But like Captain Gazzara pointed out, we need to move the needle one way or another here. Do you have any idea where Gabe might be?"

"I don't know," he breathed out in exasperation. "I don't even know where he lives. I always pick him up at work—"

My gaze snapped up to meet his. "Work? Where does he work?"

"The lumber yard," he replied. "He's a mechanic there. That's how we met. I don't have a cell. Or, I do, but I can't afford to pay for minutes." His cheeks reddened in embarrassment, but it wasn't an unusual situation for guys who'd spent years—more than a decade—in prison. "When I want to get hold of him, I just show up—"

I stood up. So did Corbin.

"Thanks," I said. "I'm sorry we had to bother you. Let's hope it's for the last time."

He nodded and walked us to the front door, and we all stepped out onto the porch. Samson, who'd been lying down with the coonhound and beagle, got to his feet.

"Lyon & Holmes?" I asked, just to be sure.

Rogan simply nodded.

"Okay," I said. "We're heading that way now. If you hear from Corewall, you need to reach out to us."

I handed him my card with my direct line.

He nodded again. He looked weary. Corbin thanked him for the coffee, and we headed back to the SUV.

"How did we miss this?" I snapped as I yanked the rear door open. Samson leapt up onto the back seat, and I attached his collar to the seatbelt anchor, much to his displeasure.

"I don't know," Corbin said as he closed his door and I thumbed the starter button. "We knew Nathaniel worked there, with Dan Thomas and the other kid..."

"Chase Richards."

"Yeah. But I don't remember ever hearing Gabe Corewall's name being mentioned."

"Well, damn it, someone should have asked. Cooper and Dani have been looking for him for days, and they said they checked where he worked, but I don't remember them mentioning where that was. Hell, all this time and he could've been right in front of our noses." I was mad at myself for missing that detail. *What a total waste of time and energy!*

And now, Rogan was running out of time. Johnston was breathing down my neck, and I had the feeling it wouldn't be long before he ordered me to bring him in, proof or not.

34

Thursday morning, 11:00 a.m.

THE LYON & HOLMES LUMBER YARD WAS BUSY, bustling with activity; busy enough that I'd decided to leave Samson in the car.

It was raining again. Just a fine drizzle, but enough to make me uncomfortable as we walked across the yard to the makeshift office.

The door was ajar, so I knocked on the doorframe and stepped inside. The office was empty, aside from a desk, a computer, a file cabinet, and a chair with a scruffy-looking guy seated thereon. A grimy window offered a clouded view across the yard to the main building.

The scruffy guy at the desk was small and reminded me a little of Danny DeVito but not nearly so charming. His hair had obviously been artificially dyed a dark brown, almost black, and his beady eyes peered up at us as we entered.

"What do you want?" he barked, glaring at our badges, his mouth twisted in distaste. "You cops have been showing up here almost every day, disrupting my yard, my workers. If this continues, I'm gonna reach out to the mayor."

I ignored his rambling discourse and stepped up to the desk.

"We're here about one of your employees," I said. "Gabe Corewall. Where is he?"

The man snorted, stood up, came around the desk and tried to get in my face. Or rather, my chest.

"Gabe doesn't work for me," he snapped.

Corbin, not liking how aggressive he was, stepped up beside me with his hand on his Glock.

"Step away from the captain," he said in a tone that brooked no argument.

He did, his hands up level with his shoulders, palms out, and said, "Okay, okay. I got ya."

"We were told he works here as a mechanic," I said.

"He does."

I took a deep, slow breath in through my nose. The man was trying my patience.

"All right," I snapped. "That's enough. We know he works here. So where is he?"

The man smiled, revealing a mouthful of yellowing teeth, a couple of them oddly pointed. "I told you. Gabe Corewall doesn't work *for me*. I just manage the yard, okay?"

"Then who does he work for?" Corbin snapped. The manager eyed him aggressively, despite being almost a foot shorter than him.

"He works for a third party. We contract them."

I could feel my blood pressure rising. "Listen to me," I said. "If Gabe Corewall is on this property and you fail to tell us—"

"What?" he snapped, puffing out his chest. "What're you going to do, hun? Sic the rest of your cops on me? Go ahead. Try it!"

I slipped my hand around to the back of my belt and grabbed my handcuffs, more than ready to take the guy, when a voice spoke up from the door.

"Sal, what's going on?" It was Chase Richards, victim Jared Moore's older brother. He stepped inside, his hard hat crooked, dripping water from the rain. "Are you crazy? Just tell them where Gabe is." He'd obviously been listening.

The little manager scowled and said, "I don't know where he is."

Chase shook his head and then looked at me and said, "Gabe's off for the next two weeks. He's staying with his sister in Spring City. She's having a baby."

"Did you know that?" I asked, fingering my handcuffs and looking at the man we now knew as Sal. "Because if you did—"

"I didn't," he snapped.

"So he's on PTO, personal time off?" I asked, and Chase shot Sal a nasty look.

"Well, I don't think he was approved for PTO, but if that's where Chase says he is, that's where he'll be."

"Do you, by any chance, have the sister's name and address?" Corbin asked Chase. He sounded as frustrated as I felt.

"Charlene. Charlene Corewall," he said. "She's not married. I don't know the address, but it should be easy enough to find, I guess."

"Thank you, Chase," I said, snapping the cuffs back in their pouch and gesturing toward the door. And we stepped outside, ignoring Sal as he angrily shuffled binders and paperwork around on his desk.

Once outside, in the rain, Chase said, "Sorry about that. We get a lot of visits from the police, mostly because of the type of people we have working here. Sal's kind of bitter because his brother was arrested a few years ago on a domestic violence charge, so he's not exactly looking to help y'all out."

"He came pretty close to getting arrested, himself," I said. "But thanks again, Chase. If you happen to hear from Gabe, have him call me, please," and I handed him one of my cards.

"How well d'you know him, by the way?" I asked.

"Not well," Chase said. "He's a good mechanic, and he keeps things running around here, and that keeps the bosses happy, you know?"

"I do," I said. "Thanks again."

"Any word on who killed Jared?" he asked, almost casually.

"Nothing I can share," I said. "Sorry."

He nodded, turned away and headed off toward the main building. Corbin and I ran back to the SUV, my hair wet, the water dripping off my leather jacket. I felt thoroughly miserable.

"I don't like this," I said as I settled down in my seat and slammed the door on the rain. "It's taking way too long, and we still have no idea who the killer is. And I have this awful feeling we're missing something; that the answer is right in front of our noses."

We talked for a minute or two, waiting for the interior to warm up, then Corbin said, "There is one good thing, I suppose."

I looked at him. "There is? And what would that be?" I asked, skeptically.

"Well, there haven't been any more shootings since Monday night."

"Oh, for God's sake, Corbin," I said. "It's only Thursday. Geez. You think maybe the killer's taking a couple of days off? You pray there are no more, or we're done."

35

Thursday afternoon, 1:00 p.m.

FINDING CHARLENE COREWALL'S ADDRESS HADN'T been difficult. A quick search on the DMV database was all it took.

"I need you two to go to Spring City," I said to Hawk. "Talk to Gabe Corewall and try to confirm Rogan's alibi. Get a signed statement, one way or the other. Take it easy. It's an easy run up Highway 27, but the roads are wet."

He looked at me as if to say, *Are you kidding me? I've been driving these roads since before you were born*, but instead, he said, "No problem, Kate. We'll head out in a few."

I nodded, and Samson and I, now dry and warm again, headed to the elevators, the door to which closed just as I received a text from Corbin.

You sure you're good to go by yourself?

He was referring to my decision to visit Ben Whitt once more. I was bothered that all signs still pointed to Nathaniel Rogan. I knew that even if Hawk and Anne were able to confirm his alibi, Johnston wasn't about to let go of Rogan. I figured that, knowing Corewall owned a gun, he'd want to rope them both in.

Me? Something about Ben Whitt was bothering me, eating away at me like an itchy mosquito bite.

I'm good, I replied to Corbin as I settled in behind the wheel, knowing that the alone time would be good for me. I didn't need him getting tangled up in my hunt for Ben Whitt, anyway. The less he knew about my little adventure, the better.

I sighed and looked up at the rear-view mirror to see Samson's serious face looking back at me.

"Where to, do you think, Sammyo?" I asked, waiting for a second as if the dog would actually respond. "Yup! That's what I was thinking, too," I said as I put the unmarked SUV in drive and pulled out onto Amnicola and headed for the ranch, hoping that Whitt would be at work.

It was just after one in the afternoon when I turned into the driveway and drove toward the house/barns complex.

The intricately carved sign reading Silver Waters was impressive, and once again Sammy kept his eyes on the horses.

I drove slowly, hoping not to draw attention to myself; hoping to catch Whitt off guard.

Up ahead, I saw a figure cross from one barn to the

other. The doors to the building he entered were open, and from what I could see, it looked like a stable, and the figure looked like Luke Webber.

Well now, I thought. *Isn't that convenient?*

I parked back near the fence line, maybe fifty yards away from the barn, where several other vehicles were parked. And then I sat for a moment and considered my options.

And then I saw it. Parked next to a shed, half-hidden, about halfway between me and the stable, was a black pickup truck with dual rear wheels.

"You stay here, boy, and guard the car," I said, ignoring his sad whine.

I got out, closed the door quietly, and sticking to the grassy strip alongside the fence, I approached the truck. I wanted to get a good look at that sucker.

The truck was parked at the side of the shed facing an empty field. I started with the truck bed but found nothing of interest, just the usual stuff: a toolbox, a loose spool of fishing line, a worn pair of work gloves and boots, and some bright yellow straps.

I glanced around, feeling kind of stupid. I was, after all, a captain of detectives, and though I had no right to be searching the vehicle without a warrant, I told myself I wasn't touching anything, just looking. Yeah, right!

Anyway, the yard was still quiet. There was no sign of Whitt, though I heard the snort and stomp of a horse somewhere, probably in the stables.

I made my way around the truck to the cab and

peered in through the back window of the truck—and saw a rifle lying on the back seat.

I nodded, self-satisfied, and smiled to myself. By then I was between the truck and the shed, where no one could see me.

I stood up on the balls of my feet and peered in through the driver's side window. I could see a soda can in the cup holder in the center console, along with some loose change. There was a beanie on the dash, and I could see the rifle on the back seat.

On impulse, I tried the door handle. It was locked. But that rifle. I could see it was a lever action, but I couldn't see the brand.

Knowing that with my car and Samson out there in the open I was pushing my luck, I gave it up and walked back out around the shed and headed for the stables.

While I still hadn't found Ben Whitt, I figured I could kill some time by asking Luke Webber a few questions.

The stable was huge; a central walkway, at least thirty feet wide, stretched from one end of the building to the other, bounded, by my count, by twenty-four horse stalls on either side, most of them occupied, for a total of forty-eight. Silver Waters was a serious operation.

It wasn't exactly dark inside, but it wasn't exactly well lit, either. But it was warm, and, I supposed, cozy for the horses therein. *What does an operation like this cost to run?* I wondered as I slowly walked down the center of the walkway.

I heard a loud thump just a few yards away to my left. A little startled, I turned and looked. A huge white head was gazing at me over the open half door. I stepped up close and stroked the soft white muzzle. He huffed, nodded, turned his backside to the wooden wall and snapped his right hind hoof back against it, making another loud thud.

"Hey," I said, smiling at him. "Are you trying to intimidate me?"

He whickered and shook his head, then nudged me with his nose. I scratched his hard forehead and walked on, slower, paying attention to the other stalls. The majority were occupied; most of the horses were munching away at their hay or seemed to be napping with their eyes half-shut.

I found Luke Webber mucking out the third to last stall on the right.

"Hey, Luke," I said, giving him a heads-up.

He jumped and yanked a single headphone out of his left ear.

"Oh, wow. Uh... Hi," he stuttered.

I nodded, then said, "Remember me, Luke? I'm Captain Gazzara. I was looking for Ben Whitt.

"He's around here somewhere," he replied. "Not sure where, though."

"D'you have a few moments?" I asked.

"Sure," he replied and leaned on his pitchfork. "What can I do for you, Captain?"

"Well, as you probably know, we've spoken to Ben a couple of times. I was hoping to talk to him about his relationships with Caroline Davis and your cousin, Lindsey Waller."

"O...kay," he said, frowning.

"How did they get along, Caroline and Ben?"

Luke shrugged and made a face. "They argued now and then, like most couples do, right? But yeah. They got along fine, I guess."

"Do you recall what those arguments were about?" I asked.

"You know," he said, "I don't feel comfortable talking about him behind his back."

"I understand," I said agreeably. "I just thought you might have a little insight, is all. What did they argue about?"

Luke glanced to the left, where the rear exit was, as if he was expecting him to walk in at any moment. Then he sighed, shook his head and said, "Okay. It was just... well, I think Caroline thought Ben was a little too... clingy, like, you know?"

He flushed, obviously embarrassed to be airing his friend's secrets.

"And Ben thought she flirted too much with other guys." He paused, then added. "She had a lot of guy friends. Hey, she was a good-looking girl, right?"

"Hmm. Okay," I said. "Did he feel the same way about Lindsey? Was she flirty too?"

Luke frowned, looked annoyed and said, "Hell, no. Lindsey's a good kid. She'd never cheat or flirt... She's strong-willed, yeah, but she's, like I said, a good kid." He smiled at me.

"You must be upset about what happened to her, and Daniel," I said gently, returning his smile.

He shrugged again, his shoulders slumped, and he looked down at the muck. And kicked it, "Yeah, I mean. Poor old Dan got shot in the head. Lindsey? She got lucky, I guess. Sounds like the guy wasn't such a good shot, maybe."

"She told you about what happened?" I asked. I wasn't thrilled with the idea of Lindsey talking to anyone. The last thing we needed was for the public to know the details of what had happened.

Luke shook his head. "Nah. Her mom told my mom. My mom told me. She said Dan got shot right in the forehead. That's... rad, man." He eyed the exit again. Somewhere far off, a lawnmower started up.

"That it is," I said. "I'm sorry, Luke. I hope she's doing okay." He nodded solemnly, then sighed.

"Anything else you want to ask, or can I get back to work?" He picked up the pitchfork and stared down at the floor.

"Just a couple of things," I said. "It won't take but a minute. I understand that Ben had a hard time with the breakups. Did he ever strike you as aggressive? Or violent?"

"What?" he snapped. "You think Ben is up for this? No frickin' way."

"I didn't say that," I replied and then waited.

He frowned, then said, "I mean, we played football in high school, right? So yeah, I've seen him be aggressive. But with girls?" He looked at me and rubbed the back of his neck, squinting. "Nah! Well, I guess, maybe a little... not aggressive; not really. I mean, more like... well, he has a bit of a temper, like, you know? But he means well. He really does. He wouldn't hurt a fly, really."

"So what kind of things upset him?" I asked.

"Well, I don't know, do I? Disrespect, maybe? He gets that from his dad, I think," he added, smiling. It was clearly a joke, but it hit too close to home. I didn't return Luke's grin, and it faded quickly.

"He gets mad when he misses a shot when we're out squirrel hunting, or when Jimmy here—that's the ranch manager—gets on our asses about something. Sorry, didn't mean to cuss. He gets mad when they get his order wrong at Mama Luke's, and he gets mad at his dad's dog... sometimes. He doesn't like dogs..." He trailed off after rambling out a surprisingly long list of items. His next smile sat awkwardly on a tense jaw. "Look, I don't like talking about him, okay?"

"And he gets mad at girls, too?" I asked, watching his eyes.

"Well... yeah. I suppose. Don't we all?" His eyes were wide. "I've seen him argue with Lindsey, but I've never seen him... like, get mad or hit them or anything."

The sentence ended lamely again, not exactly inspiring confidence. I straightened up, took a deep breath and said, "Thanks, Luke. I appreciate you trying to be helpful."

"Can I..." He gestured to the pitchfork and wheelbarrow, and I nodded, turned away, and walked toward the rear exit. I got about halfway, then turned and said, "And you don't have any idea where he might be?"

He stood upright, a fork full of muck in his hand, and shrugged. "Dunno. Like I said, he's around here some-where. But it's a big ranch."

36

Thursday afternoon, 2:15 p.m.

I DIDN'T HAVE ANY LUCK FINDING BEN WHITT THAT afternoon, despite his truck being there. Luke was right. It was a big ranch. I checked in at the main house, but no one came to the door. Other than that, I only ran into two other workers. One didn't speak English well enough to understand what I was asking, and the other told me I'd have to talk to Jimmy, and the way he said it, it came across as a warning. Not that I gave a damn by then. I was frustrated and beyond tired.

After twenty minutes more searching fruitlessly for Jimmy and Ben Whitt, I finally gave up and decided to return to the PD and... talk to Chief Johnston.

IT WAS JUST after two-fifteen when I parked the car on the front lot outside the department. I got out, put Samson on his leash and let him out, set my jaw, and together started toward Johnston's office.

"Sit down, Kate," he said, not bothering to look up as I walked into his office. "I hope you have good news. Tell me you have someone en route to pick up Rogan and book him."

"Nope," I said casually, sitting down and crossing my legs at the ankles. Samson settled down next to me, sitting up straight and proud.

Johnston glared at me over the top of his desk. "What are you here for, then? I told you I wanted this wrapped—"

"Chief," I interrupted him, ignoring the flash of warning in his eyes, "You need to hear me out. We need to talk this out. I know you're set on Rogan, but—"

"Kate, if you mention Ben Whitt *one more time*."

We were at a standoff, staring at each other, neither of us breaking.

Finally, I said, "You're going to have to trust me, Wesley." I think that was only the second time I'd used his first name in all the years I'd worked for him. "There's no way you're going to be able to hang it on Rogan," I continued. "He has an alibi for the night Lindsey and Daniel were shot. We found Gabe Corewall. He's in Spring City with his sister. She's having a baby. I sent Anne and Hawk up there to see him only a couple of hours ago. Anne texted me. He confirmed Rogan's story. They were together from nine-thirty till after one in the morning, coon hunting, just as Rogan said. They were nowhere near Highway 58. *It, wasn't, him."*

Samson, sitting next to me, huffed, and I tried not to grin. Johnston's face was set like granite; it wasn't the news he wanted to hear.

"But I did get to talk to one of Ben Whitt's friends again today. And I got a look at his truck. It has dual rear wheels, and there was a lever action rifle lying on the back seat. You want to hear this?"

The chief sighed, putting down his pen. "All right, Kate. You have my attention."

"Well, I talked to Lindsey Waller's cousin, Luke Webber. He's also Whitt's best friend. Apparently, he, Whitt, has a temper, especially where girls disrespecting him are concerned. And he dated both Caroline Davis and Lindsey Waller. And, they both dumped him."

Johnston's jaw worked as if he was chewing on something. "All right," he said. "So Whitt's an angry teen. So what? So was I. And why shoot the boyfriends, too? And *how* did he miss Lindsey Waller?"

"Because he's a lousy shot," I said. "Webber told me that, too, and that he gets pissed when he misses. They go squirrel hunting."

"So why not finish off Lindsey, too?" he asked.

"Hell, I don't know, do I? I can't read minds. I just follow the evidence..." I trailed off. I could see by the look on his face that I'd gone a bridge too far, and he was totally pissed off.

"Get out, Kate, and take your dog with you. And

don't come back until you have something solid. You hear me?"

"What about Whitt?" I asked.

"Do what you have to but be damn careful. That father of his is an animal. Now, go!"

I nodded and stood up, feeling somewhat vindicated. I knew he was pissed at me, but he often was, and he always got over it. I got away with a lot that others wouldn't, including my arc nemesis, Henry Finkle, because I got results.

And so I pushed the chair back a little harder than was probably necessary, and I left with Samson trotting at my side.

Barely had the door closed behind me when my phone buzzed.

"Gazzara."

"Kate, it's Anne. We're on our way back, but I wanted to call and tell you anyway. Not only did Gabe Corewall confirm that he was with Rogan, but he also has GoPro video to prove it. We're bringing a copy back with us."

A slow smile spread across my face, and for a moment, I considered marching right back into Chief Wesley Johnston's office.

"That's perfect, Anne. Thank you so much. I owe you two a meal for this."

I hung up and looked down at Samson, and I swore his eyes sparkled as if he knew.

"Why not?" I asked mischievously, and I turned around, opened Johnston's door and stepped inside.

He looked up, his eyes narrowed, and he said, "Damn it, Kate. This had better be good."

"Oh, it is," I said. "Guess what? We have Rogan and Corewall on camera. They weren't anywhere near highway 58 that night. They were in Prentice State Park."

I felt a certain kind of glee in the sour look on Johnston's face as he took in the news. And it was worth every second of the last six days.

Now, maybe Sammy and I could finally get a little peace. If only for a little while. I still had a killer to catch.

37

Friday morning, 9:00 a.m.

AND SO THE WEEK ROLLED ON.

On Friday morning, by nine o'clock, I had my entire team assembled in the conference room with the reports and files related to the case spread out across the table.

"So what are we looking for again?" Jack North asked, looking up at me.

"Anything that might move the case forward," Corbin replied with a slight roll of his eyes. "Anything to do with Ben Whitt."

Sergeant Tracy Ramirez was seated next to Cooper, her designated partner, eyeballing Dani, who was seated on the opposite side of the table. Dani was focused on the task at hand; Cooper was focused on Dani, and Tracy was taking it all in.

Apparently, no one had mentioned Cooper's interest in his pseudo-partner to her. Tracy was older than

Cooper by almost two decades and was protective of him. They had this sort of big sister/little brother thing going on.

"I have to say," Anne murmured, flipping through my write up on my conversation with Luke Webber. "It isn't looking too good for Ben Whitt."

"But why does the Chief want us to take it easy on him?" Tracy asked. "Shouldn't we be bringing him in?"

"His father's a prominent, hard-nosed lawyer," I said. "That's why. He just wants us to be sure before we make a move on him."

"But you saw a rifle in his truck," Anne said. "We should get a warrant for it and run it by ballistics."

"Why can't we just pull it over?" Dani asked.

I stared at her. So did Jack and Corbin. Hawk nodded, smiling.

"We could, but we can't search it without probable cause," Ramirez said.

"Right," Hawk said, leaning forward and resting his meaty forearms on the table, "but if we catch him in a traffic violation, speeding in a residential zone, maybe, and that weapon is still unsecured on the rear seat, that would be reason enough, don't you think?"

I thought for a moment, then slowly nodded and said, "We can give it a try. Jack. Book out an unmarked cruiser from the motor pool, and you and Dani go to his house and sit on it. He comes out in that truck, you follow him. If he makes a wrong move, pull him over and take a look, but be careful. I'm not ready to take on his dad; not yet."

Jack nodded, and he and Dani left.

That was on Friday morning. Almost four days later, by five o'clock on Monday afternoon, we were no farther forward.

———

It had been a long weekend, and an even longer Monday.

It was just after five that afternoon when Corbin and I met Anne and Hawk out in the parking lot. They'd been tailing Whitt all day and they looked worn out, thankful to be heading home to their families.

"Anything?" I asked, already knowing the answer.

Anne shook her head. "Sorry, Kate. Nothing today."

After four days of almost nonstop surveillance, we'd sighted the black F-350 only a couple of times on Friday. But Saturday, Sunday, and apparently Monday, we'd not seen hide nor hair of it. The red truck; yes.

I drive whatever I want, whenever I want.

"All right," I said, looking to Samson with his sadly wagging tail. "You ready to go, partner?"

Corbin looked at me, frowned and said, "You talking to him, or me?"

I smiled at him as I opened the rear door for Sammy and said, "Get in the car, Corbin. We've another long night ahead of us."

38

Wednesday evening, 7:00 p.m.

SAMSON AND I HAD MOVED INTO THE NEW HOUSE over the weekend, and by Wednesday, I'd pretty well gotten the place straightened out.

I'd left work at lunchtime to do some final shopping and, that done, I'd taken Sammy for a walk and we were on our way home. *Our Home. I never thought I'd see the day.*

It was December 11, and just after four-thirty in the afternoon, late enough in the afternoon that people had their lights on. I had to admit, I loved the amber glow of the suburban neighborhood, though I still wasn't used to the lack of the constant noise of the traffic on East Brainerd Road or the smell of fast food, but I was enjoying the peace and quiet.

As we reached the driveway, Samson tugged toward the gate that led to the backyard. He *loved* that yard; he lay stretched out in the sun whenever he could, and when he couldn't, he sat and stared out the French doors.

"No. Not now, Sammy," I said. "We have to eat dinner."

By seven that evening, I'd showered and was unashamedly in my pajamas. I was tired and frustrated, wanting nothing more than a mind-numbing evening in front of the television with a glass of wine, perhaps two, and then a good night's sleep.

The case had reached a dead end. We had no new leads, and I didn't dare bring Ben Whitt in for questioning without probable cause. The only good thing about it was that Chief Johnston had finally backed off Nate Rogan.

"It just *has* to be Whitt," I said out loud as I dumped my backside down on the couch next to Samson, continuing the same one-sided conversation I had several times a day for the past several days. *With a dog*, I thought. *I must be going out of my tiny mind.*

I'd called off the surveillance. It had been wearing us all out and getting us nowhere.

And, of course, Chief Johnston was giving me a hard time; the press was having a field day with our lack of progress.

As I sat there that evening, watching reruns of *The Andy Griffith Show*, I couldn't help but wonder what must be going through the killer's mind.

"At least there aren't more victims," I muttered and looked at Samson. He stared silently back at me.

"Some partner you are," I said. He tilted his head sideways and stared up at me.

I patted him on the head and watched as Barney hitched up his belt and told Andy they had to nip it in the bud, a sentiment I totally agreed with.

But, for whatever reason, the killer had quieted down. Was it because the killer had gotten what he wanted? Yes, I was convinced it was a he, and that I knew who he was. Had he only targeted the two couples because the two girls had dumped him, disrespected him? Or was it because he knew we were onto him and had gone to ground?

But something wasn't sitting right in my gut.

It had been eleven days since Daniel Thomas had been shot dead and...

It was at that moment something occurred to me. I frowned. *How did he know... How, did, he, know? I need to call Cindy Davis!* And I did, and two minutes later, barely after I'd ended the call and was sitting there, trying to make sense of what she'd said, my phone rang. Startled, I grabbed it and looked at the screen. It was dispatch.

"Sorry to bother you, Captain. We have a shooting out on Highway 58, near Booker T. Washington State Park."

"Got it," I snapped. "What info d'you have on the victim, or victims, anything?"

"Not much, ma'am. Only that there are two."

"Alive?"

"As of right now... yes."

"Give me the coordinates," I said. "I'll be there in twenty."

I ran to my bedroom, stripped off my pajamas, hauled on a pair of jeans and a white roll-neck sweater, slipped into a pair of sneakers and then into my shoulder holster. I checked my Glock, slipped it into the holster, grabbed my keys and pointed at Samson.

"You," I snapped. "Let's go."

I was halfway out the door when my phone rang again. It was my partner.

"Corbin! You get the call?"

"Already on my way, Kate. I'll see you there, unless you need me to swing by and pick you up."

"Nope. I'm good. This might be it, Corbin. I know who the killer is, and it's not Ben Whitt. And this time he messed up. Both victims are still alive."

"Yeah. I heard that," he said. "But if it's not Whitt, who is it?"

"It's Luke Webber," I replied.

"Luke Webber?" He sounded stunned. "How did you come up with—"

"I don't have time for that right now," I said, cutting him off. "I'll tell you later. Right now, we need to get out there."

Two minutes later, Samson and I were in my SUV and headed out on Highway 58.

39

Wednesday evening, 8:15 p.m.

THE SCENE WAS CHAOTIC, WITH MULTIPLE CRUISERS parked haphazardly both on the road and along the hard shoulder. Samson's collar jingled as he jumped out of the back. An officer held out a hand for his leash, but I declined, wanting to keep him with me. Just in case.

An ambulance was parked almost horizontally near a Rav4. One quick glance in the blinding red-and-blue lights was all it took for me to see the driver's side front tire was flat.

"Hey," I called, getting the attention of one of the paramedics. It was Charlie Roper, one of the regulars I knew quite well. "I'm told you have two. Are they alive?"

He nodded but looked grim. "Yes, one, a girl, is in bad shape. Collapsed lung. She's on the way to the hospital. She's the one who called 911. This here is—"

Before he could tell me more, I heard someone shouting. It was a male, and I knew by the sound of his voice who he was.

"I'm going to kill him," he screamed. "Lemme out of here. I'm gonna frickin' kill him."

He was lying on the gurney inside the ambulance. Two paramedics were working on his thigh. His blood-soaked boots were on the floor.

"Hello, Ben," I said. "What happened here?"

He looked at me, wild-eyed, anger lighting him up like a firecracker.

"He shot me," he snapped, "so I shot back, okay? That son of a bitch has got my gun." He pointed to a uniformed officer standing close by holding a shotgun.

"No one's frickin' listening to me," he shouted. "He's still out there, in the woods!"

"Luke Webber?" I asked.

He nodded.

"Tell me what happened," I said. "Be quick."

Something was telling me we didn't have a lot of time.

"Mattie and me, we were out here for... well, you know, a hike."

Yeah, that, I thought.

"We got out here maybe an hour ago," he said. "We were just about to pull out of the parking lot when we noticed she'd gotten a flat."

"This is her car?" I asked.

He nodded. "Yeah, so we got out to change it. And then Luke showed up. The son of a bitch is wearing camo, and he has a gun. He shot Mattie, and then he shot me and ran off. Ouch!" he yelped, flinching away from the paramedic.

"So while I was getting my gun out of the back, Mattie must've managed to call 911. Luke must be still out there, in the woods." He nodded toward the dark line of trees. "He's in the woods."

I backed away from the ambulance and stared at the trees, the forest. So, Luke Webber was out there somewhere, with a gun, wearing camo. *Geez, that's just great.*

40

Wednesday evening, 8:30 p.m.

I LOOKED AROUND FOR CORBIN. HE WAS TALKING TO one of the two officers who were first to arrive on the scene. I joined him.

"...didn't see anyone?" he asked, looking from one to the other. I looked on as they both shook their heads.

"Nothing," the senior of the two said, "just the two victims."

Pulling Corbin aside, I told him, "Whitt says he's still out there, in the woods."

"What're you planning, Kate?" he asked.

"Ben," I said, turning back to the ambulance.

The paramedic was wrapping his thigh. He looked pale, scared.

"Which way did he go?"

"That way." He tipped his head to the right.

I looked at Corbin. He nodded. I went to my car and

grabbed two flak jackets—body armor—and handed one to Corbin. We put them on. I checked my Glock, then turned again to Corbin.

"You ready?" I asked.

"As much as I can be," he replied.

I nodded and said, "Let's go."

I turned Samson loose, and we were about to head out down the road when:

"Hey," a uniformed lieutenant shouted. "Where the hell d'you two think you're going? This is an active scene. There's a shooter out there."

I didn't know him, and he obviously didn't know me, or Corbin.

I turned around, flashed the badge on my flak jacket and said, "Captain Gazzara, homicide. Stay back and control the scene."

"But..."

I ignored him, and Corbin and I started out down the road at a swift jog, Samson loping on ahead, weaving this way and that, his nose close to the ground. He stopped for a moment, then disappeared into the darkness, to the right.

"Oh shit," I snapped. "Samson, come here, boy. Sammy, come." I looked at Corbin. "Damn it," I said. "I should have left him in the car."

We walked on a few yards to the place where Samson had disappeared and realized it was a service road. Overgrown but still in use.

"Webber must've gone that way," I said. "To get to his truck. Come on." I drew my Glock, and together we walked into the darkness, toward the trees, and I could feel the skin on the back of my neck crawling. *If he has a night vision scope...* It didn't bear thinking about.

I could feel the mud sucking at my sneakers and cursed myself for not taking the time to put on my boots.

Far off in the distance, back along the road at the crime scene, we could hear shouting and car doors slamming, and I figured Mike Willis and his team of techs must have arrived.

Hell, it wouldn't have surprised me if the chief was also on his way.

I glanced behind me. We were now out of sight of the main road, maybe as much as a quarter mile in.

"Hey. Stop. Listen. Look," Corbin whispered.

"What?" I whispered. "I can't see anything..." And then I could. Maybe twenty yards ahead, its wheels deep in the mud, was a black truck, its engine running.

It was literally the end of the road, and bad luck, for Luke. In the light of Corbin's flashlight, we could see a huge log jammed tight under the front of the truck.

With our weapons low, we circled around the vehicle and approached it from the front, from either side. Corbin lit up the interior with his flashlight. There was no one inside.

"Oh... shit!" I said and rolled my shoulders, again feeling the skin on the back of my neck crawling. "Where the hell is he? He can't be far. Where the hell is Samson?" I didn't dare call him. I didn't want to attract our killer's attention.

"Ben was right," Corbin whispered. "He must have taken off into the woods."

"What are we going to do?" Corbin asked.

"I think it would be wise if we split up," I said. I sure as hell didn't want to. You have no idea how scary it was, out there in the dark with a killer on the loose, with a high-power rifle and wearing camo. The odds were all in his favor. There were game trails everywhere, and it was anybody's guess which one Luke had taken.

41

Wednesday evening, 9:45 p.m.

WE'D BEEN OUT THERE FOR ALMOST AN HOUR WHEN I heard the thumping of a helicopter overhead. I looked up and saw the beam of its spotlight slicing through the darkness. It found me, stopped moving, holding me in its beam. I waved upward. It moved on again, sweeping back and forth across the tops of the trees.

I knew that by then, other teams were out searching the hundreds of acres of woodland, and I found out later that even the park rangers had joined in the search.

By then, though, my thighs were burning from the effort I was putting in, plowing through the mud, pushing through undergrowth, and clambering over rotting logs. It was a different beast from a flat, ten-mile run on smooth pavement.

The light from the chopper momentarily broke

through the canopy, and I got a glimpse of the path ahead of me; if you could even call it that.

And then the woods began to clear; big, tall pines taking over from the heavy brush and spruce, the thick carpet of pine needles muffling my steps.

Unfortunately, they also muffled Luke's. I wanted to catch him; oh yes, but I didn't want him to catch me. *Where the hell is Samson?* I thought for the umpteenth time.

How had I known it was Luke Webber? It was while I was sitting on the couch at home that it hit me: how did he know that Daniel Thomas had been shot in the forehead? We hadn't released the information. Only the killer could have known that. He said his mother had told him, and that Cindy Davis, Lindsey's mother, had told her. That's why I called her. Cindy said she'd told no one, and that's how I knew. Luke was the killer.

I shook my head and tried to concentrate on the task at hand, to focus on my surroundings. The last thing I needed was to be caught out in the woods with a gun trained on me. And I knew that Luke Webber was better than an average shot.

But my mind continued to run away with me, recalling the conversations I'd had with Luke. How casually he'd leaned against the pitchfork. His easy grin. He'd seemed like a genuinely okay guy, a young kid with manners and a little sassiness.

A shiver went up my spine as I considered just how deranged Luke Webber must have become. And then I heard it. Somewhere nearby, a twig snapped.

I stopped dead, went completely still.

42

Wednesday evening, 10:15 p.m.

I SWUNG MY GUN AROUND IN A WIDE ARC, UNNERVED by the laughter echoing among the pines. The sound of search helicopters was far off, and it sank in just how alone out there I was. Corbin had gone off on his own. Samson had disappeared more than an hour ago, and I was so damn scared I...

"Luke!" I called. "Is that you? Come on out and let's talk this thing through, okay?"

Bang!

Something hit the barrel of my Glock, wrenching it from my hand and sending it spinning away into the undergrowth, leaving my hand numb and my nerves tingling. I was stunned. I mean, utterly stunned. To make a shot like that, at night, in the dark. It was impossible.

But it wasn't. He did it. It was only later I learned his rifle was equipped with a Pulsar N750 Digisight.

Instinctively, I ducked and put up my hands. Where the hell was Samson? I was filled with fear at the thought of Luke Webber shooting my dog, and I hoped the stupid thing had done the right thing and had gone running off to safety, back to the crime scene.

And then Luke stepped out from behind a large pine tree. I couldn't see his face in the shadows, but I could see the 30-30 rifle was aimed right at my chest.

"Hell...o, Captain," he said. "Just to be clear, I have no problem shooting you. And I'm well aware that you've come further into the woods than anyone else. There's no one coming to save you. It's just me and you. Isn't that nice? Cozy, even?"

The guy was a complete fruit loop.

"They won't be reaching us anytime soon," he added.

I had my hands up, my palms facing out, and I was sweating, despite the cold night.

"Luke, I—"

"Get on the ground," he snapped.

I hesitated.

"Do it now, or I'll blow a hole through your chest."

Slowly, I lowered myself to my knees. The thick layer of pine needles was soft underneath.

Luke took a couple of steps closer. The rifle now pointed at my head.

"Why'd you do it, Luke? You're obviously an amazing shot. Why didn't you kill them—Lindsey, Ben and his girlfriend?"

Luke sneered, the shadows turning his frown into

something horrific. "Doesn't matter," he said in a low voice.

"It was because Lindsey's your cousin, wasn't it? And because Ben was your best friend?"

"Lindsey's an idiot," he said. "Always with a different guy. She couldn't just be happy with what she had."

I frowned. "You mean Ben? You were upset because she broke up with him?"

"Ben's just as bad," he said. "He runs through girls like they're tissues. He's beyond stupid. Mattie deserves better."

"And what about Ben?" I said. "He was your best friend, the one person in the world who was close to you. Now he says he wants to kill you. Now you have no one."

"I already had no one," Luke snapped. The silence was deafening. "I've had no one for months now," he whispered. "Ben's an asshole."

"Bullshit," I said. "You have Lindsey, your parents, your job."

Well, not anymore, not after murdering three innocent kids.

"I had Stephanie," he said wistfully.

Stephanie? The name didn't ring a bell. Who the heck was Stephanie?

Toeing a thin line, I tried to find a compassionate way to ask...that wouldn't earn me a bullet to the brain.

"Who's Stephanie?" I said. "What happened to her?"

The muzzle of the gun dipped, just for a moment. And then he began talking in a rush, as if the words had been locked inside and the door had burst open.

"She was my girlfriend," he said. "We dated for two years. And she was perfect; everything I could have asked for. She was going to go to Vanderbilt for sociology, and I was going to tag along, get a job, get an apartment. So we could be together there. But—"

He choked on the word, the rifle dipping down again.

"What happened, Luke?" I asked quietly.

"She died." He swallowed audibly. "I took her out on my bike for a date, and there was an accident."

"Accidents happen," I said. "It's not your fault she died—"

"I was driving," he snapped, cutting me off. "I was the one who took the corner too quick. Steph wasn't wearing a helmet."

I winced. But needing to move the conversation past his grief, I asked, "Your bike?"

"I drive a truck now," he said.

"So..." I said hesitantly, "so when Stephanie died, that was it for you? That's not how it works, Luke. I know it's hard, but you get over it eventually. You can be happy again—"

"I can't," he barked out. "And no one else can, either."

It was hard not to roll my eyes. That was a cliché, but it wasn't difficult to understand, though it was a stupid reason to go on a killing spree.

"So why did you only shoot Lindsey in the arm, then?" I asked, refusing to believe that he could have missed her.

"I don't kill family," he said. "Besides, my aunt would never forgive me."

"Ben and Mattie, though—"

"I didn't know he was dating Mattie," he said, cutting me off. "Ben has the worst taste; she's only sixteen. Did you know that? And she's a slut."

I was about to reply when I saw a dark shadow moving slowly, silently through the trees behind him; a shadow I recognized instantly. It was hard to miss those big ears.

So, instead of replying to his spurious remark about Mattie's character, I took a deep breath and tried to calm myself. The next few seconds were going to be crucial.

As I watched, I could hear Webber rambling on and on, trying to justify his killing spree, but none of it sunk in. My attention was on the shadow as it crept slowly forward.

And then... my phone rang. Webber almost jumped out of his skin as the warbling ringtone echoed through the trees.

Samson bounded forward, leapt into the air, and his front paws, backed up by a hundred and fifteen pounds of body weight, hit Webber square in the middle of his back. He was thrown forward, arms in the air. The gun went off. He landed flat on his face. The rifle flew out of his hand and landed several feet away. Sam whipped around him, seized his upper arm, and clamped down with his jaws. Webber screamed.

I jumped to my feet, scrabbling for my cuffs; the damn things were missing.

Samson was going to town on his arm, shaking his head, growling, Webber screaming. I leapt forward, but my foot slipped on the loose and slippery pine needles. I pitched over sideways, rolled, scrambled up onto my knees and leapt onto Webber's back, grabbed his flailing free arm and wrenched it up behind his back. I knelt, my knee firmly in the middle of his back and shouted, "Samson. Off!"

He released the arm immediately and backed off a couple of small steps, stationed himself in front of Webber's face, head down, ears flattened, growling, teeth bared, and he wasn't smiling. Webber froze, transfixed by the sight of those huge teeth only inches away from his face.

I wrenched his injured arm behind his back, and sitting straddled across his back, I held his wrists, one in each hand, pressed against the small of his back, wondering what to do next. I couldn't let him go, or should I say I dare not let him go.

Breathing hard, I looked at Samson. "You took your damn time."

He looked at me and licked his lips.

Fortunately—so I thought at the time—it was only moments later I heard the sound of people crashing through the undergrowth. Or rather, a person. Corbin made a surprising amount of noise. He appeared like a noisy wraith, grabbing my attention.

Samson leapt to his feet and spun around, instantly on guard.

Webber rolled to the side, pitching me off his back. He grabbed me from behind, his arm around my neck, pulling me in front of him, reaching for the rifle. Samson turned again and leapt forward.

"Samson, down!" I screamed as Corbin took aim and fired.

Corbin was a good shot, and the bullet hit Webber in his left shoulder. He fell back, screaming, with me on my back on top of him and Samson growling in his face.

Corbin ran forward, grabbed my hand and hauled me to my feet. I staggered back a couple of steps, then stood bent over, my hands on my knees, breathing hard, watching as Corbin snapped the cuffs on Webber.

"Samson, heel," I said as Corbin stood up and turned to me.

"You okay, Kate?" he asked.

"Yes, I'm fine," I said, reaching down to scratch behind Samson's ears.

He nodded, thumbed the talk button on his radio, and called in the coordinates.

It was over, all but the shouting.

43

Wednesday evening, 11:00 p.m.

I WATCHED AS TWO UNIFORMED OFFICERS LED Webber away through the trees, back to the service road and from there to a waiting ambulance.

In the light of more than a dozen flashlights, he looked pathetic, a shadow of the hard-ass he professed to be. Someone had made a makeshift pad and stuffed it under his shirt to slow the bleeding. He looked grim, tired, beaten, his face streaked with tears and dirt.

Me? Corbin and I followed. I was limping. I'd jammed my knee pretty hard when I fell, and some fifteen minutes later, sitting against the hood of a cruiser, I gingerly moved it back and forth, wondering if I should join the party at the hospital.

"Hey," I called to Corbin, who was going to follow the ambulance. "When you get there, make sure you take the long way round. Don't let Ben Whitt see him, or he'll try to kill him," I joked.

Corbin grinned. "No love lost between friends, huh?"

"Kate." Chief Johnston appeared at my side, taking in my disheveled appearance and the mud caking my clothes. "You all right? You certainly look like you took down a killer."

Looking over his shoulder, I caught Mike Willis' eye. The bald man nodded, a silent note of approval, and I nodded back. "I'm fine," I said. "Though I could do with a shower."

I could feel dirt in my ears, and it was driving me crazy.

The chief looked down, eyeing Samson, who was sitting quietly beside me, seemingly oblivious to all the noise and lights and cameras; yes, the press had arrived in force.

"I heard this guy got involved, too," Johnston grunted.

"He took him down," I confirmed. "If it hadn't been for him, Webber would have killed me."

Johnston smiled, reached down and scratched Samson's ears, and said, "Can't be too bad of a mutt then, can he?" Then he scratched Sammy's head. The dog abandoned his dignified demeanor, closed his eyes and whined his approval.

"Did he talk to you at all; Webber?" Johnston asked.

"Oh, yes. He played the victim. It sounds like this whole thing was prompted by his girlfriend's death a few months ago. He blames himself for it. But it wasn't just that. He has some sort of complex. I... I don't know. He didn't like the way his friends—if you can call them that—flipped from one relationship to another. He called Whitt's girlfriend a slut. He's obviously grieving, and I think it must have triggered... something. I don't know, Chief. I'm not a shrink."

Johnston nodded, obviously deep in thought. "But why shoot them from a distance?"

I shrugged. I didn't know the answer to that either. "Maybe he thought he wouldn't be discovered. No evidence at the crime scenes."

"We got word from the hospital a few minutes ago," he said. "The girl—Mattie Green—will be okay. She'll be in for a couple of days, but they're expecting a full recovery. And Ben Whitt is doing just fine, too. He'll be discharged tonight into the care of his parents."

"That's good." I pushed off the cruiser, wincing at my bruised knee. "Chief, if it's okay with you, I'd like to head home and get a shower."

"Of course. Well done, Kate. I'm proud of you." He smiled, staring at the top of my head. I reached up. It was caked with mud. I grinned back at him.

"Thanks, Chief," I replied.

He nodded. "Go home and rest. We'll talk in the morning." And, with that, he turned and walked away.

"Come on, buddy," I said to Samson. "Let's go get cleaned up." He was even muddier than I was.

44

Sunday afternoon, 1:00 p.m.

My new house was beginning to feel like home.

I hadn't realized just how much that mess of a case had put me off, kept me unsettled and on edge. But by the time I sank onto the couch in the new living room that following Sunday afternoon, and Sammy jumped up beside me, pretending he wasn't breaking the rules, all of the pieces had clicked into place, and I was looking forward to a quiet Christmas.

Samson huffed and put his head on his paws, his eyes trained on the TV as if he was actually paying attention, and I lay back and closed my eyes, thinking back over the past couple of weeks. Had it only been that long? It seemed like half a lifetime.

Webber had been arraigned on Thursday morning on a litany of charges, including three counts of first-degree murder and three counts of attempted first-degree murder. He'd appeared in court completely alone; no family, no friends. Apparently, even his mom had abandoned him when he'd graduated high school. He'd been right when he told me he was all alone, and I couldn't help but feel kind of sorry for him. He tried a plea of insanity, but it was thrown out after two independent psychiatric evaluations, and he eventually stood trial for his crimes. After a short, two-day trial, he was found guilty on all charges—the jury taking only forty-eight minutes to reach a verdict—and he was sentenced to life in prison without the possibility of parole.

But that was all yet to come. As I sat on the couch and sipped my wine that afternoon—part of the reward to myself and my four-day vacation of self-care and recuperation—I couldn't help but wonder what would have happened if we hadn't caught him when we did. Would more lives have been lost? There was no way to tell, but I knew if they had, I would've blamed myself.

Webber hadn't once asked about Lindsey, Mattie Green, or his one-time best pal, Ben Whitt, and that surprised me. After all, he'd been genuinely worried about his cousin.

My biggest failure, so I thought, was the black truck. We'd—no, I'd automatically connected it to Whitt. That was bad. As a seasoned detective, I should always assume nothing. I should have run the truck. Had I done so, I would have quickly learned it belonged not to Ben Whitt but to Luke Webber, and the case might have—would have—taken a completely different direction, so I blamed myself for that.

And, looking back, Luke had always been somewhere around. They worked at the same place, him and Whitt. He must've driven Ben to the ranch that day I saw the rifle in the truck.

"There was no way we could've known any of that, though, could we, Sammy?" I murmured. "I guess in a weird sort of way, we got lucky. If Luke hadn't slipped up that day when he was talking to me... If... If... And then you took him down, didn't you, boy?"

Samson lifted his head, tilted it, opened his mouth and let his big old pink tongue fall out, and I laughed and patted his head.

"But don't get too used to the good life, Sammy. I'm sure the phone will ring soon enough."

THANK YOU FOR TAKING THE TIME TO READ CAROLINE. THE SIXTEENTH BOOK IN THE SPIN-OFF SERIES OF NOVELS FEATURING LIEUTENANT KATE GAZZARA. THE NEXT BOOK IN THIS SERIES IS IN THE WORKS AND WILL BE AVAILABLE IN THE SPRING OF 2023.

WHILE YOU WAIT, CHECK OUT JOKERS WILD FROM THE HARRY STARKE NOVELS.

JOKERS WILD: THE HARRY STARKE NOVELS BOOK 18
AVAILABLE IN eBOOK, PAPERBACK, & AUDIO.

Genesis - "As always with Blair Howard's books, there are lots of dead ends and twists and turns . . . Great read!"
Alice - Online Reviewer

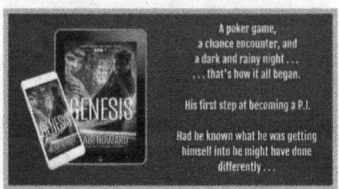

Would you like to get a free copy of the first book in my best-selling Harry Starke Genesis series?
Visit www.blairhowardbooks.com

THANK YOU

Once again, I'd like to thank you for reading **Caroline.** If you liked it, perhaps you would consider posting a short review (just a sentence will do). Word of mouth is an author's best friend and much appreciated.

To those many of my readers who have already posted reviews to this and my other novels, thank you for your past and continued support.

VISIT MY WEBSITE AT
WWW.BLAIRHOWARDBOOKS.COM.

From Blair Howard

The Harry Starke Genesis Series

The Harry Starke Series

The Lt. Kate Gazzara Murder Files

The Peacemaker Series

The O'Sullivan Chronicles: Civil War Series

From Blair C. Howard

The Science Fiction Sovereign Star Series

ABOUT THE AUTHOR

Blair Howard is a retired journalist turned novelist. He's the author of more than 40 novels including the international best-selling Harry Starke series of crime stories, the Lt. Kate Gazzara series, and the Harry Starke Genesis series. He's also the author of the Peacemaker series of international thrillers and five Civil War/Western novels.

If you enjoy reading Science Fiction thrillers, Mr. Howard has made his debut into the genre with, The Sovereign Stars Series under the name, Blair C. Howard.

Visit www.blairhowardbooks.com.

You can also find Blair Howard on Social Media

COPYRIGHT